Acclaim for Maureen Gibbon's

SWIMMING SWEET ARROW

"An amazing novel of hard lives and hard sex. Vangie Raybuck is a riveting original who goes all the way and then some — and who is able to look truth in the eye without blinking. *Swimming Sweet Arrow* is unflinching in its honesty and integrity. A wonderful debut!"
— Paulette Bates Alden, author of *Crossing the Moon*

"If a female Ernest Hemingway were contemporary and were to write a story of two young women and their raw, visceral, small-town lives, the story might well be *Swimming Sweet Arrow*."
— Kristianna Bertelsen, *Express Books* (San Francisco)

"It's exhilarating to find a fictional character who's in control of her desires — even when they lead her into dangerous territory. . . . [Gibbon writes] with an artistry as straightforward as the arrow in the title of her novel."   — *Independent Weekly* (Durham, NC)

"I read *Swimming Sweet Arrow* in one impassioned sitting. Maureen Gibbon has done something brave and intelligent — and erotic."   — Susanna Moore, author of *In the Cut*

"A startlingly candid debut novel."
— Chris Waddington, *Minneapolis Star-Tribune*

"A sexually explicit novel that's neither repulsively blunt nor falsely lyrical. For men who wonder what girls talk about when they talk about lust."   — Walter Kirn, *GQ*

"The accomplishment of *Swimming Sweet Arrow* is in the voice — an affecting blend of innocence and experience, an attempt to give words to what seems inarticulate about love. . . . This coming-of-age story is both satisfying and unexpected, an account of swimming in deep water and navigating its currents alone."
— Maile Meloy, *New York Times Book Review*

"*Swimming Sweet Arrow* is an almost crazily courageous knockout of a first novel, beautiful in its risky honesty."
— Elizabeth Tallent, author of *Honey*

"Gibbon convincingly pinpoints the unembarrassed drives of late teenhood and the curious way that such energetic openings up to love, sex, and the world can cause some major shutdowns as well."
— Mark Rozzo, *Los Angeles Times Book Review*

"As the reader tumbles through this admittedly explicit novel, the realization dawns that it is merely written in the language of sex. . . . The words and vivid description provide a racy vehicle for deeper concepts of love, life, decisions, and growing up."
— Gina Temple, *Ripsaw* (Duluth, MN)

"Refreshing. . . . The two friends' closeness and unpredictability, even to each other, is one of the best things about *Swimming Sweet Arrow*."
— Ann Ryan, *Creative Loafing* (Charlotte, NC)

"A harrowingly impressive debut. . . . Gibbon's writing is blessedly free of condescension. . . . She skillfully immerses us in this world of chicken factories and greasy spoons, of keg parties and drunken couplings. And she ultimately persuades us to care — deeply — about her unlikely but strangely endearing heroine."
— Kevin Riordan, *New Jersey Courier-Post*

"Powerful. . . . An impressive accomplishment. . . . Maureen Gibbon's first novel explores the many elements — violence, poverty, drug abuse, and religion — that can intertwine in unfathomable ways. . . . The sex scenes alone are enough to keep any hot-blooded reader turning pages." — Kara Jesella, *Nylon*

"There now it is all written down. The broken, working-class families, the sex, drugs, dead-end lives, and through it all the thing one really longs for: a true decency. Luminous, simple, tough, and written with stunning candor."
— James Salter, author of *A Sport and a Pastime* and *Light Years*

Swimming Sweet Arrow

Swimming

Sweet

Arrow

A NOVEL

Maureen Gibbon

LITTLE, BROWN AND COMPANY

Boston   New York   London

Originally published in hardcover by Little, Brown, May 2000
First Back Bay paperback edition, August 2001

"What Is This Gypsy Passion for Separation," from *The Selected Poems of Marina Tsvetaeva*
by Marina Tsvetaeva, translated by Elaine Feinstein, copyright © 1971, 1981 by Elaine
Feinstein. Used by permission of Dutton, a division of Penguin Putnam Inc.

Library of Congress Cataloging-in-Publication Data

Gibbon, Maureen.
    Swimming sweet arrow : a novel / Maureen Gibbon — 1st ed.
        p.   cm.
    ISBN 0-316-30599-5 (hc) / 0-316-35556-9 (pb)
    1. Female friendship — Fiction. 2. Young women — Fiction. 3. Young women —
Sexual behavior — Fiction. I. Title.

PS3557.I139167 S95 2000
813'.54 — dc21   99-053347

10 9 8 7 6 5 4

Q-FF

Printed in the United States of America

For my family

. . . how completely and
how deeply faithless we are, which is
to say: how true we are to ourselves.

— MARINA TSVETAEVA

Swimming Sweet Arrow

1

WHEN I was eighteen, I went parking with my boyfriend Del, my best friend June, and her boyfriend Ray. What I mean is that June fucked Ray and I fucked Del in the same car, at the same time.

The first time it happened was an accident. We'd been at a formal dance at the school, and we all wanted to go parking and kissing for a while. The speed we did — in the bathrooms just outside the gym — was still in our systems, but the whooshing of June's long, fancy dress and my long, fancy dress on the car seats drove us all over the edge. I think Del and Ray even came at the same time, what with all the rocking in the car and general excitement.

After that, we planned the nights together. Each couple still had their private times — unlike Del, I couldn't come with the others in the car — but all four of us liked the feel of the extra kissing, sucking, and nakedness going on. We went to the same cornfield each time, parked beneath the trees on the property line, and drank a case of beer. We drank and talked until, by some cue, the touching started and the talking stopped. When we fucked, Del and I didn't talk to June and Ray, and they didn't talk to us. The only sounds in the car were small groans and sighs and sometimes the slippery sound of cock moving into pussy. We used either Del's or Ray's car, and we took turns being in the backseat.

On this particular night, we were in Ray's car and Del and I had the front seat. After we screwed, I lay with Del between my legs, my knees opened as far as they could be between the seat and the dash. Two of our feet were up on the seat, and two were down there by the gas and brake.

"I can't believe we do this," June said from the backseat. I could tell from her voice that she was feeling silly. "I'm best friends with you, Vangie, and there you are."

She and I could see each other — just eyes and the tops of heads — in the space between the seat and the door.

"You broke my rhythm with all your humping," Ray said from the back to tease Del, and when we all laughed, Del slipped out of me, slip, just like that.

"Now I'm cold," I said, and meant the wet place between my legs, but Del reached down on the floor of the car and gave me my shirt.

"Cover up," he said. "I'm going to piss."

"I'm out," Ray said, and he climbed off June. He and Del straddled the car doors, legs going through the open windows. They had to climb out of the car like that because June and I never wanted them to open the doors and make the light go on. We liked to get dressed in the dark, grabbing our clothes from the floor, talking and laughing.

"Their asses look so funny when they do that," June said, and it was true. The whole side of the car filled with butt, and I couldn't stop myself from watching. I mostly watched Del, but I snuck looks at Ray, too. He had dark hair that almost looked black, but his skin was ten times fairer than Del's. He was taller than Del, and thicker through the chest, and I thought that made him seem right for June. When I squeezed June's arm when we were acting crazy or when I wanted to bug her, it was soft in a way that made me want to go on touching it. I thought holding her had to be that way, too, and that Ray would be good at it.

"They look silvery in the moonlight," I said, and June nodded. She was sneaking looks at Del, too, but like the rest of what we did together, the looking June and I did at the other's boyfriend did not seem strange or unnatural.

By the time Del and Ray were coming back, June and I had put on our bras and shirts. I watched Del walk barefoot and naked across the ground. He looked handsome. He wore his hair long in the back, and the black hair framed his face and shoulders. Because his eyes seemed half closed and because of a small, crooked scar that split an eyebrow, Del's face had a tough, lazy look that I liked. I also liked seeing behind that look when he smiled or was being sweet with me, or when he was on top of me, fucking me, and the skin around his eyes puffed up because he was moving into me so hard.

There was something good about being able to see Del naked and walking toward me. I was able to look at his face and his chest and his penis, all at the same time. His body looked like it fit together, and it seemed like a dark, natural thing. What I liked best was how dark his cock and balls were, darker than the skin of his thighs and belly. I could not stop looking at the dark, good color, and just seeing him loosened something inside me. Of course he saw me looking — I was staring — and he smiled as he got back in the car.

"So you like my cock," he whispered when he slid onto the seat beside me. His teeth were crooked and doubled back on themselves in places, and I passed my tongue hard over them when I kissed him to give him his answer. He took my left hand and moved it to cover him, to hold him, and I thought what I always thought when I touched him there: that skin couldn't be softer. It was like the skin behind your ear but even softer, and now he was damp against my hand.

"I like it," I said. I knew June and Ray probably heard the whole thing, but I didn't care. I liked that Del talked to me like that, and I liked the way his face looked when he said those kinds of things to me. He was not afraid to do things, not afraid to try things with me, with my body.

"Are you ready?" June asked.

We always went to pee together, not because we were afraid of the woods or anything, but because it was friendlier to do it with someone else. She couldn't see where my hand was, but I think she knew anyway. I let go.

"Sure, now the lights can go on," Ray said when we opened the car doors. We all laughed because he was sitting in the backseat, holding his shirt over himself. A line of hair snaked down his belly, and that's where I could see how white his skin was.

June and I walked to the first line of trees, where we could squat and pee. I even liked doing that: being outside and feeling the cool air between my thighs, the leaves and bits of dirt beneath my toes. We didn't bring tissues to wipe ourselves but stayed and air-dried a bit.

"I just leave it all here," June said to me.

"What?"

"Everything," she said. "Piss, come. It all just runs out of me."

"I know," I said. It was why we never put on more than our shirts and bras — because we knew our pussies were so wet. I liked knowing that it wasn't just piss running out of me but also Del. Something about being wet with his come made me happy in a way I didn't have words for. It made me feel wild, I guess, and like a woman — but those words didn't get at how I felt when I smelled that sharp smell or felt that slipperiness. When June and I talked about sex we sometimes used this one phrase: *young and dumb and full of come.* I didn't feel dumb, but I liked the saying because it rhymed and because it used the word *come.* I didn't wash any of it away before I went to bed, either. I might wash my feet, dirty from walking barefoot, but I'd leave that smell on me.

"Are you staying over?"

"I told my mom I was," June said.

"Good. I don't want to be alone."

"I'm someone."

"I know," I said.

I'd heard talk in school about other couples screwing together, but as June and I walked back half-naked to the car, I knew that no one could ever be like us. No one would be better friends than June and me, and no one would screw like us. What other people did inside their cars or beside the lake didn't matter. The four of us were inside our own web.

All the way out to the house, Del and I sat in the backseat. He kept one arm on the door, his hand in the open air, and one hand between my thighs. I squeezed his hand with the muscles in my legs to get him to think of the other way I squeezed him — with the muscles in my pussy — and I put my arm around his shoulders. I felt tough and older when I put my arm around him. Del was a year older than I was, and I saw him as a man, different from other guys in our grade.

"One time we'll have to go camping," Del said to me. "You can tell your dad you're with her." He rubbed his fingers over the wet part of my jeans.

"Maybe she and Ray can go."

"I don't give a shit what they do. I want to be with you."

I thought about how good it would be to sleep in a tent with him, and I smiled and made a secret sign on his shoulder blade with my fingernail — a butterfly. Sitting like that with him, I knew what I always knew after we'd been together: that it was sweet to Del, too. That's what I saw in his face when he walked back to the car and asked me if I liked his cock. He was glad I liked his body, he was glad I liked to touch him. He would never say it that way, but I knew he felt it. *Sweet, sweet,* I thought when we were driving around the lake, which was called Sweet Arrow. *Sweet arrow means straight arrow, an arrow that flies straight and true.*

"What are you thinking about?" Del asked me.

"Nothing," I said. "Just about you."

NEITHER OF my parents wanted me, so I lived by myself in a run-down apartment my dad found for me. I shouldn't say it like that. My mom offered to have me come and live with her in New Mexico, but I didn't want to change schools and I didn't want to leave Del. My dad wanted to be a bachelor again, so it seemed like the best plan for me to live on my own in the kitchenette. That was what my dad called the place he found for me. It was one room with a kitchen area and a sofa bed, and a separate little bathroom. The apartment was above a small-engine repair place on the way out of town, and I think my dad picked it because he was only about five miles down the road. He bought me groceries and checked on me once each night — to see how I was, and to make sure I didn't have Del over. I guess that's what he thought a dad did: buy groceries and be ready to raise hell.

When the four of us got to the apartment that night, June and Ray and Del and I spent a long time hanging in the windows of Ray's car, saying goodbye and kissing in the night air. After being so long outside and feeling coolness on our skin, when June and I came in, we thought the apartment seemed stuffy. We opened windows and then started pulling the cushions off the sofa bed so we could go to sleep.

"Do you think we'll get tired of it?" June said when we were folding back the blankets.

"Probably. After a while."

"Do you ever look at Ray?"

"Sometimes," I said. "When I'm looking at Del sometimes I can't stop from looking over."

"I look at Del."

"I know," I said, nodding. "You can."

She went into the tiny bathroom then, to change into her nightgown. It didn't matter that she and I had just been naked and screwing our boyfriends in the same car — June and I always gave each other privacy for getting changed. I knew her breasts were covered with Ray's hickeys, and she knew my breasts and thighs were covered with Del's. But for whatever reason, we did not come out and stare at each other.

When June came out of the bathroom, I already had our water pipe and pot out on the sofa bed.

"Do you ever think we should stop smoking so much?" she said.

"Come on. Young and dumb. We'll stop another night."

"We always say that, too," she said, and we laughed.

I didn't care. I wanted to smoke and think about Del. June sat up cross-legged on the bed while I filled the pipe with dope we'd cleaned the other night. Sometimes I thought of what it would be like to sneak Del into the apartment and sleep with him all night, but I did not want to take a chance on my father's wrath. Besides, it was all right to be sitting there with June. She was more than a friend, and more than even a best friend.

After I was high, I said, "Sometimes Del gets really deep inside me."

"Do you like it?"

"It hurts sometimes, but I still like it. It's like he's at the very end of me."

"Do you think you love him?" June said.

"I know so," I said. I held the smoke in and mouthed the words. "I love the way he feels."

"I don't know if I love Ray."

After she said it, she touched the little place at her hairline where the pigment broke. There, just beside her part, her hair was not deep brown but was as blond as mine.

"What do you mean?" I said.

"I don't know what I mean."

I kept waiting for her to say something else about Ray, but she didn't — she just went on fingering that little strip of pale skin and light hair. Though I didn't know what she was thinking, I thought she seemed sad, so I kept us smoking until we finished two bowls.

We peed one last time, and I flicked in a Cars tape that would play, over and over, all night. On a night when we had been smoking and drinking, I kept the tape player on because weed made me nervous and fractured my sleep. If I woke up, the sound and the green lights of the tape player would keep me company in the dark until I could sleep again. And I knew I would wake up, because even as I was lying there, trying to let sleep come, I found myself worrying.

In spite of how much I loved to party, I worried about how all the drugs I did were affecting my body. I was secretly sure they had changed me forever. I also worried about how Del and I would get a place of our own after graduation. All of Del's money went into his car, and every time I saved something, I'd blow it on weed and booze. Of course, my worries would have been solved if I ever stopped smoking and speeding and drinking, but it never occurred to me to stop, because it wasn't really my life that I wanted to change — I just wanted not to worry.

Though I wasn't sure if it was real or not, as I lay there I thought I could feel a little achy place inside my vagina, sore from screwing. In half-sleep I felt June move on the bed and then felt her leg lightly pressing against mine. Sometimes when we accidentally touched, we moved immediately away from each other. Other times, we'd let our legs stay touching or let our backs rest against each other. That night June didn't move and neither did I.

I watched the green lights of the tape player for a while, then closed my eyes. The whole time I could hear June's breathing and feel the little bit of weight on my skin that was her resting against me. I kept finding those things in the darkness.

2

H ERE is what they never tell you about being a girl. The lucky few will crack the nut after a time or two, but the rest of us will screw for a long time before we get it right. A long time. I screwed for four years before I came. You tell that to any guy, he'll shit. They get it from the start, and go on getting it and getting it. It takes a girl longer to figure out how to get hers, because if she isn't one of the lucky few who spill it on a cock, she's got to get it in a way that doesn't hurt the boy's feelings. Try that when you're fucking in the woods or a car, or when everyone tells you that you're only screwing because you want love. You don't even know you're supposed to come.

I first screwed a boy when I was thirteen, but I didn't come until three boyfriends later, with Del. He made me come when we were sixty-nining on a dirty bunk in a cabin we broke into, out in Mennonite Town. It was all the licking and sucking that did it. When those contractions started, I didn't know what they were. That's how ignorant I was about my own body. My mom never said a word about any of it, and the clinic in Ontelaunee where I got my birth control pills made you learn about your fallopian tubes and your ovaries, but as for the rest, as for pleasure, you were on your own. They didn't even teach you the names for your labia and clitoris — nothing that wasn't connected with reproducing.

It was a shock to me that the inside of me could feel so good and loose, and I had to get Del's cock out of my mouth so I could make the noise that came out of my body. I think I cried out from being scared as much as from the feeling.

"It's like that toy with the rings," I told Del when I got my breath. I knew he didn't understand what I meant, and that almost made me cry. I was thinking of that toy where colored rings of different sizes rest on top of each other, all on a wooden dowel. Take away the peg and the rings begin to fall. But it is good to let them tumble, roll away, the red going one place, the blue somewhere else.

I tried again. "It's like rain," I said. "It's like you make my body rain."

He listened to me and he let me kiss his mouth over and over. His face was wet with me — chin, nose, cheeks — and

I kissed away as much of it as I could. I liked the way it tasted, sweet and salty, not bitter at all.

"Vangie moisture," he said. "I read about girls coming before."

"Where?"

"Skin magazine. No one ever came with me before, though."

He moved down so he could lie with his head on my belly and play with me. He put a finger up inside me. "You got all tight. Your pussy got all tight."

"Oh yeah?"

When he moved away from me, I thought we were going to start screwing, because he still hadn't come. But we didn't. Instead, he got the flashlight he'd used when we'd broken the lock on the cabin, and he shined the thing between my legs. He pulled at me, holding the flashlight in one hand, moving my lips apart with the other. His fingers were gentle, but they kept tugging. I knew he was studying me, and I had to close my eyes from nervousness. My whole body felt hot even though the air in the cabin was cool.

"Pussy looks complicated, but it's not," Del said then. "It's about as complicated as an eyelid."

It took me a second to understand what he meant, but then I got a picture in my mind of the inner corner of the eyelid with its little bud, and the way the two little lips on my vagina came up to meet over my clitoris. I'd seen it how many times in the mirror I propped between my spread legs, there on my apartment floor.

Del put his flashlight away then. This time when he got between my legs, he pushed my knees up to my chest and licked me in one long lick, bottom to top.

"I'm going to know every inch of you," he told me.

I didn't say anything. There wasn't anything to say. But that's when I fell in love with Del. If it seems like a strange reason to fall in love with someone, you're wrong. Think how good it feels when the other person's mouth is on you there, how loved you feel. If the other person will not do that for you, what else won't they do?

3

AFTER Ray, June, Del, and I started screwing together, the four of us got jobs at Noecker's chicken farm, carrying and packing chickens. The jobs weren't steady — we worked after school and on Saturdays, and only when an old flock had to be taken from their cages, or when new chickens were brought in. Even though we were two couples, we never worked that way. June and I carried chickens, and Ray and Del loaded or unloaded trucks in the coop yard. We still saw a lot of each other. Old Man Noecker didn't care what we did on our breaks or what we talked about when we were loading the trucks, just so long as we moved his chickens.

This is how the job worked. In the coop, a puller yanked the chickens from their cages to hand off to June and me, and we in turn brought the chickens through the coop and out to the yard. She and I carried the chickens by one leg each, hanging upside down, three to a hand. In the yard we swung the birds up in bunches to Ray and Del so they could stuff them in slatted, wooden shipping crates that were stacked on a truck. All of it was hard work, but it was not so hard that we couldn't mess around a little as we worked. Each time June or I came out to the truck, Ray or Del had something stupid to say to us: *Do you need a rooster in your hen house? Let us know when you want a cock.* It was endless.

The old chickens were big, and sometimes a bird got its wings broken when a puller took it from the cage. Other birds had wings and feet growing onto the bars of cages, and the pullers had to yank those chickens like all the others. By the time they were handed off to June and me, the birds were usually too stunned to do anything, but every once in a while we got a chicken who acted up, who tried to peck us or the other chickens. If I had a free hand, I did what Del taught me to do the first night of work: I punched the chicken's head.

I didn't want to have anything to do with the punching at first. I thought it was the cruel kind of thing only a boy would do to an animal, like sticking a firecracker in a cat's ass just to see it blow. I tried to quiet the chickens by shaking them a little and holding them against my legs, but it wasn't enough.

"Just go ahead and hit the damn thing, Vangie," Del told me when he saw me having trouble.

"Won't it hurt them?"

"It stuns them, that's all. They're too stupid to feel it."

I thought the chickens were stupid, too, but I also thought the last thing they needed was somebody punching them in the head. Still, one panicky bird could cause such a fuss that I'd have to drop it, and that meant chasing through the liquid shit of the coop to catch it. After I had to do that a couple times, I started punching. I know I crossed over some kind of line on the second night of work when I bumped a whole handful of chickens against a wall to quiet them. Del laughed when he saw me do it.

"I had to," I said. "I didn't have a free hand to punch."

"Don't worry. They're fucking birds."

Still, I thought a lot about the chickens as I carried them. Their legs felt skinny through my gloves, and I knew it would be easy to break their bones with just my hands. The whole bird was a thing people could break apart and eat. Not for me, though. From the time I started working at Noecker's, I stopped eating chicken. I couldn't bring myself to have anything to do with eating chicken meat off chicken bones.

The jobs at Noecker's were fashionable. A lot of kids from school worked there, and going to work was almost like going to a party. It didn't matter that we all smelled like chicken shit or that we looked foolish with bandannas on our heads. No one could escape the smell, and we wore the bandannas to keep the specks of dried shit floating in the coops from settling in our hair. We didn't think about the flecks of shit we breathed into our lungs — people didn't worry about things like that back then.

Noecker's was such a social thing I even had a special outfit picked out for work: Lee jeans with straight legs, an old pair of cowboy boots, and a flannel work shirt with a few buttons open so the scoopy muscle T-shirt I stole out of my dad's drawer showed. The T-shirt was low-cut, thin, and clingy, and I knew Del could see my bra through it. My breasts were 36D, up from 34B in the last year, and I thought they were my best shot at being pretty. I still hated when people called them tits, and I left the room when my old man called me a cow, but I wanted Del to look at them. I loved the way his hands and mouth felt when he was kneading me and sucking on my nipples, and I wanted him to think of that when he was working. Because no matter how much I worried about the chickens, it wasn't birds that I thought about when I was working, it wasn't the three-fifty an hour that I was earning, and it wasn't the ever present stench and shit of the coop. It was skin.

When Del squatted to tighten the belts holding down the wooden crates, I liked to watch his jeans pull tight over his legs. When he took the chickens from me, I liked to watch his forearms twitch with the effort. Below his cuffed-up shirt, veins crisscrossed over the muscle, under the smooth skin. Only guys had forearms with thick, raised veins showing like that. Something about seeing those veins carrying the blood to and from his hands made me wild.

One night I got so aware of Del's arms and hands it seemed like he was touching me every time I came out to the truck, even though he wasn't. When we finally got a break and went out back of the coop — where you went if you wanted to make out or smoke some weed — I pulled Del's cuffs further up his arms and put my mouth over one of the raised, blue veins. I could feel its soft shape when I pushed at it with my tongue.

"Vangie," Del said after a bit and pulled me up so he could kiss me.

"I can't help it."

"You don't have to help it. I like it."

Usually when we stood against that wall, we did what all the other couples back there were doing: we'd kiss and Del would rub my nipples through my shirt and I'd stand hard between his legs so I could feel his cock through his jeans. That night those things weren't enough. When he moved his hand to one of my breasts, I sighed into our kiss.

"You like that?"

"It's like being at a party," I said, because that's how dizzy and breathless I felt.

We kissed some more, then he moved his hands to my jeans. When his fingers found the little tab on my zipper, I said, "Del, wait."

I think he thought I was going to say no, but all I did was lean back against the wall at a different angle so he could get at me. When he slipped his hand inside the elastic band of my bikinis, I tried to move further up the wall. I could feel the concrete scraping my shoulders through my shirt.

"Can I come to your party?" Del asked.

I thought it was the best thing to say, and I knew I'd have to tell June about it. For a second I thought of his chicken hands going inside me. Then I didn't care, didn't care, didn't care.

IN MAY, after we got rid of the old flock, we had to bring in a new one, and the whole procedure for moving chickens was reversed. June and I picked up chickens from Del and Ray, carried them into the coop, and handed them off to a stuffer, who put them in the cages. Since the new chickens were young and light, we had to carry four birds in each hand instead of three. It was hard to get a handle on the extra legs and control eight birds, but I still liked unloading better than loading. The new chickens were clean and tidy. They didn't have missing eyes and broken wings, and their feathers were still white instead of being soiled with the shit of the coop.

The second night we were unloading the new flock, they were short of stuffers and Old Man Noecker asked June and me if we wanted to move into one of the rows and stuff the cages.

"Want to, Vangie?" June asked, and I knew what she was saying: if we were stuck in a row, we wouldn't get to see as much of Del and Ray. But I'd never done that part of the job, and I wanted to try, so I said, "Sure. We'll see them at break."

Stuffing was a hundred times better than carrying. With one hand you held a bunch of four chickens, and with your other hand you took each chicken by its legs, pointed its head at the cage opening, and slipped it in. The whole thing was so easy that I started feeling like I was tucking little white pillows into little wire houses.

Because the new chickens didn't fuss, it was easy for June and me to work at the same pace and talk as we worked. We started gossiping about a girl we went to school with who'd refused to have sex until her boyfriend put a pre-engagement ring on her finger. This week she'd finally shown up at school with a ring, and now she was driving us all crazy with her declarations of what a good lay she was.

"Oh God," I said. "He slipped that cheap little thing on her finger and boom! She's fucking like a rabbit."

"I didn't need a ring to tell me when to fuck," June said.

I knew from other talks we had that June was more experienced than I was. She'd gone on birth control pills in the eighth grade. That was before I really knew her and before we were friends, but she told me about it. What she hadn't ever told me about was when she first had sex, so that night I asked, "When did you first do it?"

"Fool around or fuck?"

"Fuck."

"When I was ten."

She didn't look up from the chickens when she said it, and I let myself look at her for a while, and then I looked away. After a bit I said, "Who with?"

"Just someone," June said. "One of my brother Kevin's friends."

I kept my eyes on the chickens, because I did not want her to see the look on my face. I did not want her to think I judged her. All the same, I knew that when I was ten, I was a little girl in the fifth grade and about a thousand miles away from the she-cat I became by the seventh grade.

"Did it hurt?" I said. "Did he hurt you?"

"He didn't mean to. That person didn't mean to hurt me."

"What are you saying?"

"Oh Vangie. It always hurts the first time. I already had my period anyway."

I didn't say anything — I knew my voice would sound funny if I did — I just went on tucking chickens into cages and so did June. My mind was working, though. Kevin Keel was seven or eight years older than June, and his friends would have been, too. What would they have wanted with a little girl?

The whole thing was a shock to me, but it wasn't really a surprise. The stories June told me about her family made mine seem like a dream. Her older brothers were forever getting arrested for DUI, possession, and disorderly, and Kevin, the younger of the two, had served time for vehicular manslaughter. June's dad, Ty, used to lock June and her brothers out of the house when he wanted to be alone with her mom, Jeanette, and he threatened to kill them if they tried to come in. He would not let Jeanette drive or go anyplace alone, and sometimes he made her take Spanish fly.

When June told me that, she'd said, "My mom says it doesn't make you horny, it just makes you pee."

"Why does she take it, then?"

"My dad wants her to."

"Where did you go when you got locked out of the house?"

"To my grandma's. Or out in the woods."

After hearing those stories, it was no wonder to me why June always kept to herself at school. She was maybe the prettiest girl in our grade — long walnut hair with that one blond piece, eyes slanting just a bit at the corners, cheekbones so high it looked like she had sickles carved into her cheeks — but you would never notice, because she did not have good clothes and she never raised her hand to talk in class, but sat instead at a desk in back and read. She was shy at school out of plain shyness, but also because of her name. A name like that had come from years of a certain kind of living, and if her father and her brothers had made the name wild and bad, there was nothing June could do about it.

That night in the coop, I wanted to ask June more about her brother's friend, but when I turned to look at her, I decided not to. If she wanted me to know more, she would tell me. But she didn't say any more that night at Noecker's. We kept on working silently for a while, then talked about other things at school. I never heard her talk about her brother's friend again.

4

M Y mom left my dad when I was in eleventh grade, not long after Three Mile Island blew. Even though I knew there was no connection between the two events, I kept thinking there was something in the air that made her go. A cloud of recognizing, a big mushroom of knowing my dad wasn't going to change, ever.

"What did you guys fight about?" I'd asked when I saw her packing. It wasn't the first time I'd watched her.

But then, instead of saying, "Your father does not believe I deserve a seventy-nine-cent lipstick," or bitching about what time he came in the night before, my mother said, "It is never just one thing, Vangie."

When she said that, I knew she was really going and that nothing was going to change her mind. People do not usually wake up of a morning and decide to change the rest of their lives, but my mom did. A hole the size of Pennsylvania almost burned in the earth, and she never came back.

My mom gave me two gifts before she left for New Mexico. One gift was a little red jewelry box with a ballerina that sprang up when you opened the lid. It was the kind of jewelry box you gave a little girl, and my mom said she couldn't resist getting it for me.

"You'll always be my baby, Vangie. No matter how big you are or how old you get."

She even got my name engraved on a gold plate in the front of the jewelry box. *Evangeline Starr Raybuck.*

The second gift was harder to figure. In the box was a little black nightgown with spaghetti straps and a band of lace under where my breasts would be. The thing even had matching panties.

"I wanted you to have something nice," she said.

I couldn't believe it. "Shouldn't you be talking to me about being careful and not making the same mistakes you made?" I asked.

"I know you're smart, honey. Even when you were in ninth grade you were smart."

Which meant that she had found my birth control pills at some point, though she'd never said anything about them to me.

"So that's why you never had that talk with me?" I said.

"That's why. You'd already taken care of the problem."

And it was true, because I'd known all the way back when I was thirteen that I wanted nothing to do with babies. Now that I was older I felt it even more strongly. I wanted to get my pussy eaten and fucked by Del. There wasn't shit for my mom to tell me. I knew how not to get pregnant, I knew how to earn a wage, and I knew how to fuck. All my mom could do was give me a black nightie and wish me well.

My mom called a lot when she first moved, but the calls dwindled over time. She met an ex-Mormon in Albuquerque and fell in love with him and his adobe house. I understood. Her own life overtook her. I wanted my own life to overtake me. And it did. I guess I was a little out of control, though, what with smoking weed or drinking every night, speeding to go to school, and the double fucking.

My dad somehow knew something was going on. He showed up at the apartment at funny times — late at night or first thing in the morning — and asked me about four times if I wanted to go live with my mom.

"I'm saving up," I said. "I'm getting my own place after graduation."

"You always have family, Vangie. Remember that."

Yeah right, I thought. After I moved into that kitchenette, Del and June became my family. I could tell June just about anything, and though I was fucking Del almost every day by then, it was more than just sex between us.

In spite of the fact that Del's old man was as crazy as mine, and even though I knew I did not have to feel bad about my father in front of Del, I was embarrassed to have Del see certain things. One night he and I drove to my dad's house after a date. My dad was playing father that week and wanted to know what time I was getting in, so after drinking and fucking in a field for three hours, Del and I went to my dad's place so I could report in. When Del and I knocked, no one answered. The door was open, though, and when we stepped inside, there was my old man, passed out in a chair, the reek of alcohol strong in the room. It was a common enough sight to me, and I knew there was no waking him.

"Why doesn't he go to bed?" Del said when we got into the kitchen.

"He's always like that," I said.

Del shook his head but did not say anything else. Neither did I. I didn't bother to tell him about all the times I had found my father dead to the world. There was no point to telling such stories.

I wrote a note to my father that said, *I was here, 12:30 a.m. Your daughter, Vangie,* and made us walk out the back door.

Del did not make me talk about any of it. I did the same for him. I knew Del's dad was a drinker, too, and that he sometimes beat Del and Del's brother Frank — punched them hard in the face like he would grown men in a fight. But when I saw Del's messed-up face, I didn't ask him to talk about it, I just said, "Baby, can I hold you?"

With June, I still did not talk much about my dad, but when I did, she understood. Plus, I could tell her what was going on with Del and me. After June and I started fucking in the same car, we wrote a lot of notes back and forth, and they were all about sex. Neither one of us could stop thinking about it. We wrote about what we did the night before, and sometimes we played at writing outrageous stuff to each other, trying to shock, trying to be the raunchiest. Even though I never came when the four of us were together, I could write to June about coming, and I knew she knew what I meant. It was a relief and a thrill. Just that one little phrase, *young and dumb and full of come,* was enough to set off the shimmery, wet feeling in me.

Those last months of school, June stayed with me as much as she could. No one at her house seemed to care much what she did, and she knew I was lonely. Like any family, we got to have our little rituals. First we did our homework, because — surprise, surprise — we both liked getting good grades if it didn't take too much effort, and after that, we had our nightly dope session.

I loved everything about dope. My small black pipe with the gold marijuana leaf painted on it, the big black water bong that June and I bought together, the little marijuana leaf earrings inlaid with turquoise that Del bought me. In my mind those things were on par with the blue-black hickeys I wore like jewelry on my neck and breasts and thighs, or my birth control pills in their slim, pink vinyl pack. All of it was sexual. Almost every night June stayed over, we'd clean dope and roll up a bunch of joints for the next couple of days, and that was when we talked about sex. We discussed things like how the girl should move if she was on top (don't kneel or squat, but sit right on the guy's hips, your legs straight out by his chest), the best way to cover hickeys (a little bit of cover cream and baby powder, but no big scarf tied around your neck), and what spotting was (when you were on the pill and started bleeding in the middle of the month and there was no problem but the blood scared the shit out of you).

One night when June and I were cleaning dope I said, "Even my tongue is sore."

We each had a double album cover out on the table, the weed spread over the cardboard — seeds and stems off to one side, leaves to another. I always used Tanya Tucker's *TNT* album, the one where the inside picture shows her holding a bunch of dynamite and wearing that red jumpsuit. I thought Tanya was all right. She was country, but she was wild and I liked her.

"Sometimes if Ray and I kiss too hard," she said, "that little place under my tongue tears."

I handed June a plastic bag to hold open for me and poured my cleaned pile of weed into it. I knew there were things June and I didn't say to each other, and for a second the whole thing seemed too private to tell her. Then I thought, *No, June's your friend, you can tell her anything.* So I said, "It's not sore just from kissing."

"What else are you guys doing?"

We'd already smoked one joint, but I still felt shy about saying the words. But somehow I wanted to say them to her. I wanted to tell her.

"Del likes when I slip my tongue in him."

June did not say anything, and I felt like I went too far. So I did not look at her and kept my eyes instead on the weed and the seeds and stems in front of me.

"Do you like it?" she said after a bit.

"I like it," I said.

"Ray wants me to do it to him, too. I guess the two of them are talking."

"I guess," I said.

"I haven't done it yet, though."

I remembered what she told me before about not knowing if she loved Ray or not. Even though she hadn't said anything about that for a while, I didn't think she'd much like licking his ass if she didn't love him.

"It's not like a blow job," I said. "You're really, really with someone when you do it."

"But you like it."

"I like to do it and I like to have it done."

Even though she didn't say anything else to me, I knew she understood that this was another thing I'd learned and needed her to know. That was the kind of friends we were.

5

THAT June, right before we graduated, Del's mom and dad went away for a weekend for their anniversary. Del and his brother Frank divided up the nights to use the house. I wanted to stay the whole weekend, but Del didn't want to be in the house with Frank around.

"Why not?"

"I hate that son of a bitch," Del said. "I know he's going to do something and I'll get blamed for it."

The two of them were always fighting. Del had four older brothers, but Frank was the only one still at home. He was a year older than Del, and even though Del was nineteen and too old to boss around, Frank still tried to do it. Their dad ran an auto salvage yard on top of his regular job, and a lot of the work of breaking down cars for parts fell to Frank and Del. The two of them were always fighting over who should do what. Other times, whatever fight one of them was having with the old man spilled over into a fight with the other brother. Del thought his brother was a liar who would say anything to get out of trouble or make things better for himself. He wouldn't even call Frank by his name but referred to him as "you know who." When he did that, I sometimes wanted to laugh, but then I'd see the look on Del's face and I wouldn't laugh.

"Why doesn't he move out already?" I said, but Del didn't answer me.

He said, "Just be ready on Saturday," and I knew better than to make any suggestions.

ON THE big day, Del brought me out to the house around five, and we drank a six-pack and smoked cigarettes, right there in his mom's kitchen with her embroidered tea towels all around. We could have gone upstairs to Del's bedroom as soon as I got in the house, but we didn't. I think we were both trying to save that, because we knew we could fuck all night if we wanted, and because it was good just to be together in the house.

"I'm making a steak dinner for us," he told me when we finished the six-pack. "We'll eat up some of the old man's goddamn steaks."

I didn't say anything when he told me what else he was making, which was baked potatoes, corn, and Tater Tots.

They were his favorite foods, and it didn't matter to him if they were all starches. He was cooking, and I was impressed by it. I liked sitting on the hard kitchen chair and watching him do stuff. He wore jeans but no shirt, and I knew that was for me. I loved to watch his heartbeat make his skin jump, there at the base of his neck, and I loved to kiss the heartbeat place and the hollows his collarbone made. But then, I loved everything about Del — the riot of his teeth and the smell of his mouth and the color of his balls.

Del did a good job cooking. Everything came out okay, and it was even done about the same time. Still, I had a hard time even putting away half of what he served me, and in the end I had to push back my plate with most of the food still on it.

"You have to eat more than that," he said.

"If I wasn't drinking maybe I could."

"Girls are always like that. They hardly eat anything."

"I ate. My jeans are already tight."

"Give it here, then," Del said, and reached across the table for my plate. "Take off your jeans if they're too tight."

"I'm just going to undo the top button."

"Are you going to unzip them for me?" he said, and from the way he talked and the way he looked at me, I could tell it pleased him as much as it did me to be sitting at the table like that, me with my jeans open and him with his shirt off.

"Naw," I said. "Finish your dinner."

I watched him shovel the food in and he knew I was watching, so he made a purposeful show of it. He wasn't rude — he just did everything in a way that would hold my eyes. He kept looking from the plate to me, and kept his eyes on me when he chewed and swallowed. I liked watching the muscles in his jaw and cheeks move, and I kept wondering if he had a hard-on, because I could already feel the fluttering starting inside me.

When he finished the last mouthful and laid the fork on the table, he said, "You're dessert."

"What about you?"

"I'm dessert, too," he said, and put on a goofy grin. He looked like a crazy kid and he made me laugh.

When Del got up from the table then to put some of our dishes in the sink, I didn't help him. Instead I went to stand in the back doorway. I stretched both my arms over my head and leaned the side of my face and one of my breasts against the wooden door frame. Even though I had never moved like that before, something in my body knew how to do it, and I could feel in the small of my back what I must look like with my ass jutting out like that.

When Del turned from the sink to get dishes he saw me. And he came to me, just the way my body knew he would.

He pressed along my ass and my thighs, and in a few seconds he unzipped and started poking and bumping against me. I let myself feel that for a while, then I unzipped my own jeans and pushed down my panties. I didn't turn to see Del's face — I just stood on my tiptoes so he could get in me.

We fucked in the door for a long time, and though my shirt was still on, I could feel the breeze coming through the screen on the wet place between my legs. Just when my feet and calves were starting to ache from standing on tiptoe, he pulled away and said, "Jesus, Vangie, let's go upstairs."

When I turned to look at him, I saw his cock slick with me. Maybe it was because we were inside a house instead of outside or in a car, but he looked like a stranger to me just then. In the dim kitchen — the room was lit only by the light above the stove — his face was filled with shadows. He looked angry. But I knew if I could see my own face it would be serious and intent, and I figured it was wanting that was changing Del's face.

It didn't embarrass me anymore to be the one on top for sixty-nine, so upstairs in Del's room I spread my cunt open over Del's mouth and face. The more he licked me, the better it felt to have something in my mouth to suck on, but the more excited I got, the harder it was to keep my head moving up and down. Part of it felt like trying to walk on a railroad track, and the other part of it was like being underwater. I kept trying and trying, and then I couldn't try anymore, and I came.

I scooted up on the bed then and lay beside Del, ran my hand over his chest and belly. When he was lying down, his stomach scooped out under his ribs. I put my nose and mouth to his skin, licked his side and up into his armpit. He had his arm around me, and his one hand was running up and down my spine, from the small of my back to my nape. He hadn't come yet, so I said, "How do you want it?" I wanted to know if I should lie on my back or on my belly.

"I want your ass, Vangie."

I didn't say anything then. It didn't bother me that Del wanted to fuck that way, but the few times when we did it, it hurt, and I'd had to make myself stand it. It still scared me, but I wanted to do it, too. Part of me wondered why I wanted to do something that frightened me, but being with Del was about not saying no. If I said no, the next thing couldn't happen.

"Do you have some lotion?" I said.

He pulled baby oil out from under his bed. "I thought it would work better," he said.

"You have to go slow in the beginning."

"I remember."

So I lay facedown on the bed and let him oil up behind me. He did himself first, then started coating me with his fingers, slipping in one at first, then two. When he got between my legs and I felt him get ready to move into me, I reached around to take him in my hand.

"Guide me in, Vangie."

I took him in inch by inch, and when he was all the way up, I let myself start breathing again.

"How does it feel?"

"All right," I said. "Better with oil. How does it feel to you?"

"Tight as hell. Good."

He lowered himself onto me then, moving into me with his whole body. After the first few strokes, it felt good to me, too, and I knew it could happen that way: something could hurt at first and then feel good. I relaxed then and put my arms all the way out. Let Del drive me down into that bed.

DEL AND I did not fuck all night at his mom and dad's like we said we would — we passed out for a little while, then we slept off and on, both of us trying to find a way to be comfortable in his single bed. I was next to the wall, so in the middle of the night when I needed to pee, I had to crawl over Del. He woke up a little when I moved over him, but started breathing heavily again as soon as I was out of the bed. I crept downstairs and didn't turn on any lights until I got to the bathroom.

When I was done peeing and farting — it was something I couldn't bring myself to tell Del, that if he fucked me in the ass I filled up with air — I looked at myself a long time in the mirror. I was trying to see if my face looked any different, because I always thought my face should look changed as things happened to me. I was sure that spending the whole night in a bed with Del would have an effect, and when I looked in the mirror it seemed like I was different. I figured it was mostly because I looked tired, though, and because I was wearing the black nightgown my mom gave me for the first time. The black made my skin look pale.

When I turned off the bathroom light and opened the door, it took me a second to be able to see again in the darkness. When I saw a person, I thought it was Del, but it wasn't. Del's brother Frank was standing there, even though it was his night to be away from the house.

"What are you doing here?" he said.

I was going to pretend I didn't hear him, but instead I said, "What do you think, Frank?" Because of course I was standing there in his mom and dad's living room in the middle of the night in my shorty nightgown, and he knew what I was doing there.

"I guess you're fucking my brother."

"I guess," I said.

"Come here, then. I want to fuck you, too."

I thought he was teasing. Del was right upstairs and I thought Frank just wanted to get me going. I kept on thinking that even when he put one hand at the back of my neck and pulled me to him. He tried to kiss me, but I twisted my head. When he couldn't kiss my mouth, he held his face against mine and got his other arm around my waist. He hit hard across my spine a couple times.

I should have yelled then — Del would have been down the stairs in seconds — but I didn't. The whole thing caught me by surprise, and yet even as it was happening I knew that every second I stayed silent made it look like I wanted to be there.

I felt the bones in Frank's face against the bones in my face. When he used one hand to yank a nightgown strap down off my shoulder, I could see the dark homemade tattoos he had on his knuckles and wrist. He sucked and snuffled at my breast, then turned his head so he could bite my nipple with his back teeth. In a little while he tried to kiss me again. That time I let him. The kiss was hard, and I tasted alcohol when he licked the inside of my mouth.

We got on the floor, and I could feel his pubic hair scratching against me when he tried to use his fingers to push himself up inside me. He was too soft, though, and after clawing at me for a while, he gave up. We lay breathing against each other, and I could have left then but I didn't. I didn't know why I did the next thing I did — except that it seemed easier to go on than to stop. I moved down over Frank's body and took his penis in my mouth.

He stopped me after a little while. "I don't want you to blow me," he said. "I want to fuck you."

What I did was enough to get him a little harder, though, and this time when he used his fingers, he was able to push his dick inside me. It didn't feel like much of anything to me. He moved against me for about a minute, then quit. I couldn't tell if he came or not, though I doubted it. He was too soft and too drunk.

As soon as he rolled off me, I got up from the floor and away from him. In one more moment I was moving silently up the stairs.

When I got upstairs, I stood in the bedroom doorway a long time, listening to Del's steady breathing, waiting for my own breath to calm. When I could move without shaking, I passed through the air of the room and slipped back behind Del. I wrapped my arms around him, burrowed into his back. I did not let myself think of that other one moving through the house.

The rest of the night I only dozed — the same sleep I slept when I lay beside June after we had been doping. Del slept hard. He didn't move much on the bed, and he didn't wake me up in the middle of the night for sex the way he told me he would. When we did screw again, it was getting light, and we did it without talking. I kept thinking it was an angry fuck, but at the end when Del came, he said, *I love you, I love you,* and I felt shitty.

Though I couldn't believe what I'd done with Frank, I

knew part of why I did it. I knew it even that morning as I lay beside Del in the blue light. I'd wanted the thing to happen. Not the part where Frank was pounding his arm across my spine, and not the lousy fuck itself — I wanted the wanting. It was a sign of my power and my body and my effect. And when Frank kissed me, it was exciting to me because it was a stranger's kiss — except Frank was not a stranger. He was more dangerous than a stranger. I would not have chosen to fuck him if he hadn't been Del's brother. And I clearly did choose to fuck him when I took his dick in my mouth.

One other thing went through my mind when Frank started to touch me. When I watched his mouth pull at my nipple, I liked the look of it: the lips concentrating, the cheeks hollowed out a little from the sucking. His face was unfamiliar, yet it was familiar. I felt the same tug inside me as I did when Del sucked on me. There was nothing so different about it. I didn't know what it said about me that I felt that way, but it was the truth. So I let myself fuck him. It wasn't hard. It was only after, when I came upstairs to Del, that everything got hard.

WHEN DEL and I finally got up and went downstairs the next day, even after I saw for certain that Frank was gone, I felt sick in my stomach. Del started making breakfast right away, but I knew there was no way I'd be able to eat what he was making.

"You sleep okay?"

"Okay," I said, and tried to pretend I was the same person I was ten hours ago, before I fucked his brother. I went on pretending when Del and I screwed a couple last times, and when we showered together. I touched Del all the ways I knew he liked, and I wondered if that made me an even bigger traitor — because I seemed to have no difficulty with licking Del's ass or playing with his cock in the shower until he came. I could do that to Del, but I could also fuck his brother. It made me wonder what I was.

All I know is at the end of the morning, after we'd sucked and fucked, I did not feel so far away from Del. I felt terrible, like the worst kind of liar, and I knew I'd never tell Del the truth. I betrayed Del with my fucking and my lying, but those were also the only ways I could make a bridge back to him, so I chose them.

If Frank Pardee ever looked at me any differently after that night, I didn't know. I never again looked at his face or met his eyes. I never told anyone what I did, either. Not even June.

6

R IGHT after I graduated, I got a job waitressing at Dreisbach's, a restaurant there in Mahanaqua. It wasn't a very nice place and I'd never thought of working there before, but it was a job and it wasn't carrying chickens. They were willing to teach me to wait tables, so I was willing to learn.

My father wasn't crazy about me working at Dreisbach's. In his younger days, he drank in the bar of the restaurant, and he thought it was a rough place. There were always stories of fights that started there, and one of the bartenders had been killed when he tried to break up a fight between two hunters. My father said, "The only way you're going to work there is if I come to pick you up every night."

"You can't control me. I'm eighteen."

"You still live under my roof."

I didn't live in my dad's house, so what he said wasn't exactly true, but he did pay the rent on the kitchenette.

"Not much longer," I said. "Del and I are saving up. Soon I'll be long gone."

"Well, until then, you live by my rules."

To me his remarks mainly signified that I had to move, but the whole argument made me realize I was handling my dad wrong. So I said, "Okay, all right. You can come get me after work. I work until midnight."

"I'll wait for you in the bar."

And of course he was well on his way to being looped by the time midnight rolled around, and I was the one who ended up driving. He showed up two more nights after that, and then he must have figured it was too much trouble to worry about me, because on the fourth night, he told me he wouldn't come again.

"You didn't have to come in the first place. I can look after myself," I said.

He waved my comment away. "I've decided to give you the truck, Evangeline. You need a dependable vehicle if you're going to be working. I haven't been much of a father to you, but I do what I can."

I could have said, *You haven't been a bad father,* but something inside would not let me. But I did think the words, and I let myself be thrilled driving the truck back to my dad's house. Even though it wasn't the kind of vehicle I would have picked for myself, I was glad to have it. A rust-colored Ford with 87,000 miles on it.

When I pulled into my dad's driveway, he asked me for his house keys off his key ring.

"How are you going to get to work tomorrow?" I said. I didn't want him to get in trouble for his generosity, or maybe I wanted to give him one last chance to back out.

"You better go before I change my mind," he told me. Then: "You've been a good daughter, Vangie, to put up with your mother and me." Then he said, of all things, "You're a good girl."

I thought his words showed me how little he knew of me, but I was still grateful to him. I waited until my father let himself into his bachelor house before I drove away, and then I was on my own again, as always.

TO LEARN the job at Dreisbach's, I worked on slow nights with Lorraine. I knew of her before I started working there, and she knew of me because she knew my mom and dad. Lorraine had dark auburn hair that she wore in a French roll — the most glamorous hairdo I could think of when I was a little kid, and one that I still thought looked glamorous on Lorraine. She favored black-and-white uniforms, and she explained everything to me in her gravelly voice. If I became a good waitress, it was because of her.

"You never bang a plate down, honey. You set it down nice on the table. And the customer is always right. If he ordered peas and you bring peas to the table, and then he tells you he ordered corn, you just say, 'Oh my, I'm sorry,' and you take the peas back and you bring him corn."

When I told June the example of how I was supposed to admit to mistakes even if I didn't make them, June said, "You mean you don't say, 'Eat your peas, asshole?' "

"No, you're supposed to say, 'Eat your goddamn peas.' "

Of course we were high, so we laughed for half an hour about that. Yet for as stupid as I acted with June about all the Dreisbach's knowledge I was getting, I did want to be a good waitress, and I took my job seriously. I made plenty of mistakes in the beginning. Sometimes I forgot to bring silverware to a table, or I added wrong on the guest check. If I took too long getting someone's meal out to them, Earl, the cook, stood in the kitchen doorway and hollered, "Food's ready!" He bitched at me every night in Pennsylvania Dutch, and I was glad I couldn't understand him. I felt like I was working in a maze those first two weeks, but then I got a handle on the job. I learned to make all my actions as useful as possible, and I ended up liking the way the job forced me to think all the time. Once I knew, I knew, and even Earl had to stop bitching so much.

After I got accustomed to the job, though, I had time to notice more, and I became aware of how people treated me. I didn't mind the men who teased me or the women who gossiped with me — at least I was a person to them — but other customers treated me like I was some sort of lower life form. Even when they weren't outright rude, I could feel something ugly in their comments. I thought it might be all in my head, but one night I knew it wasn't. A man stood up and went to leave a dollar tip on the table for his and his wife's meal. He dropped the dollar on the floor, and when he went to pick it up, the woman said, "She'll pick it up. She'll take her money wherever she can get it."

What she said was true — I would take my money where I could get it — but I didn't know how that made me different from anyone else. I went to the ladies room and checked the mirror to see if I looked any different, but all I saw was my face. I worked in a cheap, rough place, so that was how some people saw me.

Neil Roy came in every day after he got off shift to sit at my tables. He worked in the Ringer mine in Trego, and sometimes he came in for dinner still covered with coal dust. Wherever he sat, he left that fine dirt, and I had to wipe down both the table and chair after him.

After I served him dinner for a few days, Roy asked, "Why don't you come home with me and watch me sleep?"

He had chicken gravy and chocolate milkshake in his beard, and the stink of working all day was still on him. I couldn't think of anything worse than being near him, and I didn't think what he said was funny. Roy wasn't good looking or nice, but he had big arms and a big chest from the work he did, and I guess he thought his muscles made up for his stink and his dirt. The following night, after I took his order, I got myself ready for the watch-me-sleep line, but it didn't come.

"How much for skin and how much for head?" he said instead.

I walked away. I thought he was a pig and wanted to tell him to his face, but he scared me. I believed I knew what kind of man he was. My dad had friends like that — men who were rough and didn't even know it, who used words like *cunt* and *bitch* when they talked about any girl or woman. I served Roy's food as fast as I could, but still I heard him say, "Do you give good head?" when I put his plate in front of him.

I knew I had to change if I was going to keep working. I had to learn to take people's shit and not let it bother me. So I started looking at every person who came in the door as money in my pocket, and I forced myself to make conversation. I'd lie and pretend to care how people's kids were, or I'd talk about the weather, or I'd just say, "What do you think of this crowd, now?" I said anything, just so it looked like I was friendly. I did it even with the rude sons of bitches. I did it all without meaning it, but no one seemed to care if I was just pretending. They wanted to be served by a pleasant person who brought the food while it was hot, and I don't think they cared if my friendliness was real or not.

"You see, honey?" Lorraine said after watching me operate for a while and seeing our tips go up. "It pays to be nice to people."

I knew Del and I would need a chunk of money to move in together, so I started doing everything I could to squeeze a dollar out of people. One night I sat down and hemmed all my skirts up short. I figured if men like Roy were going to say stuff to me, I'd give them something to say. After that, when I had to lean into the ice cream chest to scoop out desserts, my skirts just barely covered my ass. I took to wearing underpants over my pantyhose so that if anything showed, it was only cotton with little flowers, or nylon with a little lace. I made a couple of short, ruffly aprons, too, and I thought they added to my look. The ruffle was just enough to cover the swell of my belly, and the aprons made me look like a cocktail waitress, or so I thought. Some nights, at the end of the evening, I took my hair down out of its ponytail and let it lie long on my shoulders. I'd started dyeing it with Lady Clairol, and it was a deep golden color close to my scalp and whitish gold toward the ends. Women complimented me on the color, and men just looked. One of my regulars, an older man named Bill Mahlon, told me I looked like Veronica Lake. I didn't know who Veronica Lake was, but I could see Bill Mahlon thought I was pretty.

"She was the Peekaboo Girl," he told me. "You ask your dad."

"I don't see my dad too much."

"Oh," he said, and I knew I was getting to him: a young woman without a father. Boo hoo.

"Well, you look just like her," he said. "She wore her hair long, and it kind of hung down over one eye."

He left me a dollar tip that night and every time after, even if all he had was a twenty-five-cent cup of coffee. It was all right. If men wanted to see my long hair or my legs or the flowers on my underpants, I'd let them.

Once I convinced myself nothing mattered but getting tips, the job got better. I became a different, harder person at

Dreisbach's, and I knew that hard person stayed with me at other times, but I told myself it was good for me. Whenever I found myself thinking of certain things that I did not want to think of, I pushed them away and concentrated on the task at hand. It was not a bad skill to have, and it was the price I had to pay if I wanted to go on working. Since I did not have a choice, I decided to pay.

7

As it turned out, June moved in with Ray before I got my second paycheck from Dreisbach's. The two of them moved in with Ray's older brother. The brother, Luke, was renting a house on the road to Church's Mountain, and he invited Ray and June to go in on it with him so they could all save money on bills.

I couldn't believe it. I asked her, "Don't you and Ray want to be alone?"

"It was Ray's idea. He needs a new car."

When I told Del about it, he said, "Their bedroom has a door on it, doesn't it? Then it'll be all right."

He was right. No one was handing June or Ray a truck,

even if it did have 87,000 miles on it, and they were at least going to be together instead of just talking about it, the way Del and I did. I was probably just thinking of how I behaved with Del's brother anyway, and that had nothing at all to do with June.

In truth, I envied June living in that house. Church's Mountain was her backyard, and south of the house, private property turned to state game lands where tall pine let no sun to the forest floor. Almost every time I drove out there, I saw a hawk flying above the road or wheeling far out. And of course she was living with Ray. She got to sleep beside him all night and push back against him when she half woke from a dream or just wanted to feel his skin. As much as I loved to fuck Del in a car or on the sly at his mom and dad's house, what I really wanted was for the two of us to live together.

But June needed something to go her way. After we graduated, she went around town putting in her applications for a secretarial or typing job. Even though she'd taken the business curriculum the whole four years we were in school, and I knew from being in Miss Leader's typing class with her that she could type sixty words per minute, she didn't get one call for an interview.

"You're going to get a job sooner or later just because you have that bun on your head," I said to make her feel better, because she was even doing that: pulling all her hair, which covered her shoulder blades, into a brown donut on the top of her head.

"It's called a shin-yon," she said, and I later found out

she was saying the word *chignon,* which I never heard pronounced before. From the donut/chignon she let a few pieces sneak out so they strayed prettily around her face and the nape of her neck. I could have told her I knew those pieces were called *tendrils,* but I didn't want her to think I was teasing her about the way she talked. Even if we were country girls who fucked in cornfields, we knew how to read, and we knew words like *chignon* and *tendril.*

Even though June looked for almost a month, she could not get a job at any of the businesses in Mahanaqua. They all told her the same thing: that she should go on for more schooling, over to the business institute in Mingo County.

"Well, you could do that," I said. "You always did get good grades."

"Like I have money for it, Vangie."

She ended up doing what a lot of girls from our school did: sewing piecework in the factory. It was the one job I told myself I'd never take. I knew I'd rather listen to Neil Roy talk about me sucking his dick than sit hunched over a sewing machine every day. My mom had done it for thirteen years, and she told me it was a killing thing. So if June did have to sit sewing shirt collars all day, I was glad she at least got to go home to Ray, even if there was another person in the house with them.

I never said this to June, but I thought that if she hadn't been a Keel, if her father and brothers hadn't made the name so bad, she might have had a better chance of getting hired. But I think people in Mahanaqua heard the name Keel and figured she was one and the same with Dean and

Kevin, and no fancy hairdo was going to change their minds.

I didn't know the older of June's brothers at all, but I often saw the younger one in Dreisbach's. Kevin. He was the one who served time for vehicular manslaughter after striking down an old man on a county road. He came into Dreisbach's a few times a week for dinner. He did not let on that he knew I was June's friend, and I was sure he didn't know. He had no reason to know anything about his sister's life, judging from the distance June kept from him now. Yet that one time she talked about him, when she told me it was one of his friends that screwed her, I got the feeling things hadn't always been like that between them, and I wondered what it all meant to Kevin. Did he miss her at all? Was he sorry about letting one of his friends fuck her when she was ten? Was it why June didn't want to talk about him now?

Kevin Keel acted toward me like many of the men who came into Dreisbach's acted: he flirted with me, but he never crossed over the line. In turn, for my tip, I flirted back, but I never crossed over the line either. With all those men, what I mostly did was make a big show of taking care of their needs. When I brought their dessert or coffee, I'd set it down with a flourish and sometimes touch them — on the hand or arm, nothing more. When one of them ordered a Yuengling with his meal, I'd pour the beer for him from the long-necked brown bottle, careful to tilt the glass. It was a thing men seemed to like: someone pouring their beer for them.

"I can do that," Kevin said the first time I did it for him. "I know you're busy."

"I don't mind," I said. I tried to smile a real smile, not one of the fake kind like I gave everyone else, but it was hard because of what I knew about him.

"Working hard?"

"Hardly working," I said.

"Now that I don't believe. I seen you in here enough to know that."

I felt uncomfortable around him not only because of June, but also because I'd heard so much about the manslaughter conviction. The stories about that were rife. I heard Kevin was so drunk the night it happened, he thought the old man he ran down was a pole on the side of the road. I heard that a piece of jawbone from the old man had somehow worked its way onto the dashboard of Kevin's car. I heard that Kevin's skinny girlfriend, Sherry, was happy when he got locked up, because she could finally leave him without getting a black eye for trying. I heard that other inmates at the prison had feared him because he was always lifting weights and working out.

Still, something in me wanted to talk to Kevin Keel, and one night when I got up the courage, I sat down at his table and introduced myself.

"Your sister and I went to school together," I said. "I'm Vangie Raybuck and June's my best friend."

"Is that right? Good friends are hard to come by."

I thought I could tell by the way he held himself and looked at me that he did not want me to go on talking. So I stood up and was about to leave his table when he put out his hand to shake mine. He said, *Pleased to meet you, Vangie*

Raybuck. When I was looking at him, I could see June in his face, in the eyebrows and the shape of his mouth. He knew I was looking at him, and he let me. I imagine I wasn't the first person to study him.

I knew some of the stories about Kevin had to be lies, but I knew that some of them were probably true. Still, it was hard for me to put all those stories together with the man who sat at my tables and ate dinner quietly, who never drank more than one beer, who had my best friend's eyes and nose and mouth. But that is the nature of people, how they can surprise you with their ordinariness, and all the while a deep, powerful river is flowing through them, carrying them in whatever direction they choose to let it take them.

8

WHEN Del and I finally rented an old farmhouse out in Mennonite Town, it was a green time. I say that because it took us a good part of the summer to earn the money for first and last month's rent, plus a deposit, and because I felt like everything in my piece of the world was green and new. Del and I could fill the whole bottom of our refrigerator with beer if we wanted, we could play our stereo as loud as it would go, and we had a big bed that was always waiting for us to lie down on it. All I had to do was bump up against Del in the kitchen, or kiss his back when he was working shirtless over his car, and to the bedroom we'd go. One or two kisses and we were ready — he'd pull my lips apart with one hand and slip, in he'd go. It seemed like I was wet all the time, like the tissues down there were always swollen. In the morning Del was rock solid at my ass, and we'd say good morning by screwing, or by putting our mouths on each other. He even liked the taste of my morning cunt. We didn't speak those mornings, and sometimes we hardly looked at the other's face. I'd glimpse a brown eye when he lowered his body to mine, and because I saw it through the tangle of his hair, I sometimes felt like I was with a brown-eyed animal. I liked the feeling, because it meant I could be like an animal, too. Grunting when it felt good between my legs, running my hands over skin, pulling on the black hair that fell over the brown eye to bring the mouth down to mine.

More than just Mennonites lived in the area of Mahanaqua called Mennonite Town, but certainly Del and I were the last people you'd expect to fit in. We were as foreign as tropical birds out there, what with our drinking and drugs, Del's long hair, and the waitress uniforms I wore that just barely covered my ass. Still, that farmhouse gave us a kind of freedom we couldn't have had in an apartment in town, and I liked the place. I liked the old blue asphalt tile that covered the outside, and I liked the two old metal chairs with backs like seashells that sat on our porch. I was content.

While I liked all the sex and partying Del and I got to do once we moved in together, I also appreciated the everydayness of living with Del: being able to walk around the house in my nightgown — a comfortable cotton one, not the sexy one my mom gave me — and having someone to talk to every night before I fell asleep. Sometimes I remembered old things that happened with my mom and dad, and it often made me fretful and sick, and I was glad Del was there. Some things about my mom and dad were half funny to remember, like how we mostly ate off paper plates after they'd broken a couple sets of dishes in their fights, but most of the memories just made me sad. I wondered how the two of them got to the point where they screamed and threw things at each other. How did that much anger happen in a person? I blamed some of it on my dad's drinking, but my mom did not drink often, and she sometimes met my dad blow for blow in those fights. She was the one who split his scalp open when she threw a candy dish at him. My dad mostly used words to hurt.

"Can't you just forget about it?" Del asked me the first time I made myself sick with remembering. "You know, just push it to the back of your mind?"

"I don't set out to think about the two of them," I said. "Sometimes it just happens. You don't have to be around me if you don't want to."

"I want to be around you," he said. "I just think you should put it out of your mind. That's what I do."

But he didn't bug me about it, and sometimes when he could tell I was feeling sad, he sat with me and brushed my hair, or played cards with me until the feelings passed. Other times, if it was what I wanted, he let me be — because of course it wasn't just old memories of my mom and dad that made me fret. Sometimes I thought of what I'd done with Frank Pardee, and it goes without saying that I did not tell

Del what was on my mind then. It was my secret and I had to carry it alone.

Still, no matter how hard Del and I tried to understand each other in those first weeks of living together, it was a strange time, because everything real about life — stupid, little, everyday details of life — seemed to disappear or get complicated. We ate hamburgers, spaghetti, or bacon and eggs almost every night, because that was all I really knew how to cook. I had trouble shitting if I knew Del was in the house. And night after night, after all our screwing, I could not relax enough to let myself sleep and dream beside Del. I'd lie wakeful until three or four in the morning, when I finally would let myself drift off. Some days, depending on the shifts we were working, I stayed in bed long after Del left for work so I could catch up on the sleep I missed beside him. I told myself it was natural. I knew you could not learn everything about living with someone in a month, or get comfortable around another person in a couple weeks, even if you'd been screwing them a long time.

There were plenty of things I had to learn about Del. We kept our dope and our drugs in one drawer in the kitchen, and one of the first things I noticed about him after we started living together was that he went to work high. I used to go to school stoned or doing speed, but having to wait tables made me clean up my act. It was just too hard to weave together all the pieces of waitressing if I was stoned. If I did speed, I was great for the first part of my shift, but by the end of the eight hours, I was crashing and ready to snap. And if I went in with a hangover, I wanted to die, because

the job took so much from me physically, what with standing and walking and serving food and bussing tables and
washing dishes. So I became a weekend partyer, or I'd get
my buzz on right after I got home so that I could enjoy the
dope and still straighten up in time for work.

Not Del. Del partied hardy seven days a week, and he
made a special point of leaving time to get stoned when he
was getting ready for work. He was working a brake press at
Traut's, and I knew that job was hard: working with the
heavy sheet metal, all of it covered with oil, punching out
circuit breaker boxes all day long. I knew he hated the work,
and I knew that a lot of people on his crew partied, but I
worried about him working around heavy machinery. One
morning when he was toking up, I said, "Honey, don't you
worry you're going to fuck up at work if you're stoned?"

Del said, "No," and kept smoking. When I didn't even
get a goodbye kiss, I knew he was pissed, so I wasn't really
surprised when he didn't turn up at home that night. I knew
I was getting payback. I tried to tell myself it would all work
out and just to go to bed and get some sleep, but I slept fit-
fully, trying to listen for his car. And I thought to myself,
*Vangie, you are not going to make it if you can't sleep when he's
beside you and you can't sleep when he's gone.*

He came rolling in that night around three. When he
sat on the edge of the bed, I could smell the high stink
of the barroom on him: alcohol, smoke, the sweat of working eight hours at Traut's. It shocked me that the smell was
that strong, though I didn't know why it should. He proba-

bly smelled like that other nights when he was drinking, but I never noticed before because I was drinking, too.

I didn't care what he smelled like. When he bent over to unlace his boots, I wrapped myself around the back of him.

"Hey," I said.

"Wake up, Vangie, I want to tell you something."

"I'm up," I said.

"I'm nineteen and faster than most things on this earth. If some kind of trouble is coming, I'll get out of the way."

"What if you don't see it coming?"

"I got out of more scrapes already than the average person."

"All right," I said. "It's your business. But I worry about you."

"Vangie, they set up the press so you have to put both hands on the controls just to run the thing. Don't worry."

He stripped off his clothes and got into bed beside me, and even though his mouth was like a cesspool, I kissed him and kissed him and pulled him to me. He managed to get between my legs, then he passed out. I rolled him over on his back.

That combination of sweat and smoke and alcohol as it got pushed out of the pores — the rank odor brought back more than a few memories. From the smell of Del, you'd have thought I was in bed with my old man. That thought was so strange I refused to think it, and as soon as it came, I pushed it from my mind. I did wonder if I stank that bad when I was drinking. I didn't think so. In the old days, even when my mom sat up with my dad, matching him drink for drink, she didn't get the same smell he did. Maybe because her sweat was different, maybe she was cleaner when she started out drinking — I didn't know. It just wasn't a smell a woman could get. Or so I told myself.

EVEN THOUGH it upset me in some ways, in other ways I liked it when Del came home drunk. If he didn't just pass out, he was wildest those nights. Sometimes he took a shower because I told him how his smell reminded me of my dad, but other times he could not, or would not, wait to be with me, and I'd lie down in his stinking embrace. I forgot it soon enough, because when he was drunk he'd eat my pussy forever, or roll my nipples on his tongue and teeth until I couldn't wait to feel him move inside me. His drunkenness sometimes meant he couldn't keep an erection, but most of the time it meant he was hard for hours and still couldn't come. So he turned me out.

It was on a night when he was hard and couldn't come that we figured out a new position. Well, it wasn't a new position, but what we did with it was new. Del was fucking me and holding my feet up by his chest. He kept trying to reach down to play with my clitoris, but it was hard for him to stay up inside me when he did that.

I said, "Go on, baby. Just enjoy yourself," but he knew he was a long time from coming, so he kept trying to pluck my flower. Then the idea hit and he said to me, "Vangie, play with your pussy. Make yourself come."

So I moved my own hand between my legs. Del kept stroking, holding my ankles, turning to kiss my legs, and watching my face the whole time.

If you thought it was crazy that I didn't come the whole first four years I fucked, you will surely die when I say that night was the first time I ever masturbated and made myself come. But that was me: young and dumb.

It took a while, and I sort of rubbed myself raw, but I came that night on Del's cock for the first time. I came so hard and shook so much that Del got pulled out of his alcoholic numbness and came right after me. I was still banging my head back on the pillow when I heard him. When he finally lay his head down near mine, I kissed his cheek over and over through the tangle of his hair and I made cool circles on his back with my hands. I was happy, happy, happy.

After that night, though, I made it my business to learn everything I could about my own climaxes. I learned where to make the small circles, how to start and then stop and then start, and how, for some reason, the orgasm felt better if I hung on to the back of the bed frame with my left hand, squeezing the wood as hard as I could. As glad and as grateful as I was that I had orgasms when Del went down on me, I didn't want him to be in charge of them anymore. I didn't want anyone to have to give me my own body.

Del was into it. It turned him on to see me touch myself. I did it every time we screwed, but I'd also do it sometimes when we were sitting on the sofa watching TV, or just sitting there at the dinner table. And Del watched everything I did and dropped whatever he was doing when I spread my legs. I think I was probably like a skin flick for him, except that I was right there and real.

"Do you think you could suck my cock while you did that?" he asked one night when I was lying on the sofa, watching TV with him, playing with myself.

"I don't know. Bring it on over here."

He knelt on the floor beside me, and the sofa was just the right height for me to get him easily inside my mouth. It took a little more coordination on my part to keep everything going, but it was exciting, too. I didn't use all my terrific cock-sucking techniques, because I was concentrating on the tightness and pitch in my own body, but it didn't seem to matter to Del.

I met Del's eyes a couple of times while he was in my mouth. I had to look up over his belly and chest to see his face, and it was intense to see him from that angle. I felt like I was seeing the whole of his body. What I felt for him then had nothing to do with words.

After I made myself come, and after I made Del come, he stayed kneeling on the floor beside me. He played with my hair, moving it back from my face, running his hand from my temple to my neck, moving his fingers through the length. He played with my hair and kept touching my face and lips for the longest time, and then he said, *Vangie.*

When he said my name, I knew that he felt the thing without words, too.

9

WITH working and people's different work schedules, it was almost the end of the summer before I saw June alone. Del and I had gone out to party with her and Ray a few times, and when we finally moved into our place in August, they had come over to our house a time or two. But June and I had not had a chance to talk, just the two of us, for a long time, and one night she called and said I had to come over.

"What's up?"

"Nothing, really. I just feel like talking."

So I drove all the winding roads from Mennonite Town

to Church's Mountain, passing all the houses where, when it was daylight, I'd see wash lines with white net caps and blue shirts twisting in the breeze. When I got to June's place, before I even got out of the car, two dogs came tearing up to see who I was. I was trying to keep them off of me, and then I heard June's voice, calling them.

"They're Luke's," she said when I got to her front door. "I should have warned you."

"Where were they every other time?"

"They have a kennel out back. They're mostly friendly, but there's no way for you to know that."

Because of all the commotion with the dogs, it was the first time I really looked at her face. She seemed the same as always. That surprised me, though I didn't know why.

"Come on in. I'll tie them up while you're visiting."

When I walked in the door, I saw the Jim Beam was already on the table. It seemed strange to me only for a second. Jim Beam was not the sort of thing June and I would ever drink on our own — we were the ones who always used to want something sweet to drink when we went parking with Ray and Del. Jim Beam was the kind of thing Ray would drink, and he would want June to be able to drink it, too. I knew because Del thought I should at least be able to drink a shot of Southern Comfort, even if I didn't like it, just to show people I wasn't a candy-ass.

I had to work breakfast shift the next day, but I poured a shot anyway. I didn't want to give in to the feeling that I was getting mature about my drinking, and I wanted to keep June company.

When June came in from tying up the dogs, I said, "So, how's it going out here?"

She looked around at the old cabinets and the linoleum that was a design of baskets, and back to me at the kitchen table, and she said, "All right, it's all right."

We laughed, and I thought I knew what she meant: that nothing but nothing was what it was cracked up to be. Living with a guy wasn't all romance and sex — it was also cleaning and cooking and paying bills. At least that's what I thought her look signified, and it was my feeling that whatever made her get the Jim Beam out wasn't going to go away anytime soon.

"No, really, it's all right," she said, and she shook her head a little when she said it, because I think she knew how her face must have looked. I was expecting bad news, and I was still expecting it when she said, "Well, Ray's gone and done it."

She went to a dish on the countertop, near the sink, and picked up a ring and slipped it on her finger.

"Garnet with a diamond chip on each side," she said, and showed me the ring.

I took her fingers in mine and studied the deep red stone. It wasn't some chintzy, pre-engagement job but a real, full-fledged ring.

"It's pretty," I said, and meant it. The garnet wasn't small, and the way the ring suited June's hand made me think that Ray had spent time not only finding the ring, but also thinking about how it would look against June's skin. Or so it seemed to me.

"It is pretty."

She looked at the ring again on her hand, then she took it off and put it back in the dish on the counter.

I said, "What, don't you like it?"

"I like it."

"Why aren't you wearing it, then?"

"I do wear it. I guess I'm getting used to it."

"Is it an engagement ring?" I said. "Is that what he wants?"

"It's not an engagement ring."

"What, it's just a gift?"

"Just a gift."

But it didn't make any sense. If the ring was just a gift, she wouldn't have to get used to it, and if June liked it, she would be wearing it on her hand and would have showed it to me first thing I walked in the door.

"What are you getting used to?" I said.

"I don't know. I guess I have to get used to how much he loves me."

The way she said it, I knew she was lying. About what piece of it, I couldn't say. Maybe she and Ray were fighting and she wasn't saying, or maybe it was something else. I didn't know. But June knew I could tell she was lying, and I figured over the course of our conversation or over the Jim Beam, she'd spill the deal.

"I hemmed up all my skirts again," I said, to change the subject for a while and give the conversation room to breathe.

"Weren't they already short?"

"Well, they're shorter now," I said. "I did it for tips."

"Yeah, 'cause you really get the big tippers at Dreisbach's."

Of course, it was the whiskey kicking in, but we laughed about that, and it felt good to laugh with her. I was glad we were not talking about rings and the like.

"Naw, really I did it for me," I said. "I wanted to see my own legs. You know?"

"I know."

And I knew she did understand. The kind of jobs we had, you couldn't ever really dress up, because the work would tear apart any kind of outfit, but you had to take some kind of care of yourself, because if you didn't, you got to feeling bad about yourself. After an eight-hour shift, my hair was coated with grease from the kitchen and smelled of french fries and cigarette smoke, but at least I could look down and see the shape of my legs. With all the lifting and walking I was doing, muscles in my thighs were getting hard. Right beside the long muscle in my thigh was a little hollow. I liked seeing the shadow and shape, and I liked being at work and being able to think of the way Del's face looked when he kissed me there.

June poured me another three fingers of Jim Beam and asked how everything was going with Del, but before I had a chance to say, "He's smoking and drinking every penny he earns," the dogs started howling and she went out to quiet them.

When she came back, she seemed to forget that she had asked me about Del.

"You want to know Ray's theory about the ring?" she said.

"Go."

"He says it's all in my hands. He says he'll marry me whenever I say."

"Is that what you want?"

"I don't know."

"Well, what do you say when he asks you about it?"

"He doesn't ever ask me. He says it's like a puppy. He says if you squeeze a puppy, the puppy runs away. If you let the puppy alone, it comes."

"And you're the puppy."

"I'm the one he's trying not to squeeze."

I thought giving a girl a ring was a pretty hard squeeze, but worse was Ray trying to use dog mentality on her. I couldn't believe it. I didn't say anything, though. It wasn't mine to say. Besides, I still felt like there was something she wasn't being honest about.

"What are you going to do about the ring?" I asked.

Before she could answer, Ray's brother, Luke, walked in the room. I knew he lived there, too, but it was still a surprise to see him. He was never around those times when Del and I partied with Ray and June, and in my mind I blocked him out. I knew nothing about Luke — he had graduated before June and I even got to high school. He was an animal I knew by sight only in that corral of a town. He looked a lot like Ray — light skin and the almost-black hair — but he was thinner and his face was hawklike. Guys I went to school with got that look when they grew too fast, or when they wrestled and always had to make weight.

"You going to party with us?" I asked.

He leaned back against the kitchen counter, slouching against the wood, his arms crossed over his chest. He mostly looked down instead of looking at us, but when he did look up, when he did meet my eyes, I learned two things about him: that he wanted to be there talking to us or listening to us talk, and that he was nothing like Ray.

"Naw," he said. "If I have one, I'll want another."

"Why can't you have one and another if you want it?" I said.

"Got to work."

"He's working eleven to seven this week," June said for him. When she spoke for him, he looked over at her, not turning his head but tilting it, pointing to her with his chin and lifting his eyes to her. That fast, I knew he spent a lot of time looking at June and listening to her. I knew that because — I don't know how to say this another way — when he looked at her and listened to her, he used his mouth as well as his eyes.

"Have the rest of mine," I said, and swirled my own glass. "I promise I won't let you have any more."

"All right," he said. And I watched him unfold himself from against the counter, and I watched him bring the glass up to his mouth, his fingers over the top edge of the glass. He didn't look at June again, but by then it didn't matter. I'd already seen.

"Thanks," he said.

"Listen to him. It's his whiskey," June said, and he smiled at that.

Luke left by the back door — way too early to go to work, but maybe he didn't want to be seen by me any longer. I waited a little while, but I knew better than anybody what I'd seen. I said to June, "What, are you fucking the brother, too?"

I listened to the clock tick and watched June stare at the Jim Beam. Then I listened to her say, of all things, "Not yet. But I will."

"June," I said, and made her name about three syllables long.

"Now you know who I love."

That shut me up for a good long moment. Instead of trying to say anything, I let myself look at her in the kitchen of that run-down house on the mountain. I was surprised that she said she loved Luke, because in my mind, I thought it was just fucking. Ray was the one who gave her a ring, and Ray was the one she was supposed to be living with. I figured if she was wanting to fuck Luke, it was for the same reason I'd wanted to fuck Frank Pardee: curiosity, danger.

"You're the only one who knows," she said.

"You and Luke know."

"I mean Ray doesn't know. That's what I'm asking you, not to say."

That was the first time I thought about my role in all of it. If I knew about Luke and didn't tell Ray, I would be lying, and if I told Del none of it, I would also be lying. Ray was his friend.

"What the fuck," I said. "I can't even believe it. What about Ray?"

"I love him. I love them both."

Her voice sounded sweet. I didn't know if it was the whiskey talking or if she really thought it was that simple.

"You just got done telling me you had to get used to how much Ray liked you," I said. "Now you say you love him."

"I do love him. He's the reason I met Luke."

"Oh, Jesus. You just mean you can't have one without the other."

"Something like that. Don't be mad at me, Vangie. I wanted to tell you the truth."

We sat there not talking. I knew I had no right to say anything to her, not given what I had done with Frank Pardee. I tried to separate June's actions from my own, though, because it was her life she was speaking about, and not mine at all.

"When did it start?" I said. "When did you start up with him?"

"I don't know. Almost as soon as I moved in. It took us a long time to even kiss."

"How long is a long time?"

"Weeks. More than a month. All we did at first was talk. It's almost as easy to talk to him as to you. I even told him things about Kevin. I didn't think I ever would, but I did."

She said she told Luke how, when she was eight and Kevin had just gotten his license, he used to put a sleeping bag in the back of his old El Camino so she could lie down and look up at the sky while he drove. It used to make her dizzy to look up into the blue, but she loved it, too. She couldn't reconcile, ever, how the brother who did that for her was the same person who drove so blindly and wildly that he hadn't even known the man he hit was a person and not a pole on the side of the road. June told that much to Luke, but no more, and Luke didn't ask her to say more.

"I never told you those things about Kevin. I hardly ever talk about him."

"I know," I said. I did not ask her if she told Luke the one story she had told me about Kevin: that it was one of his friends who fucked her when she was just a kid.

"You know what he said, Vangie? When I told him I wouldn't tell him anything else, ever, about my brothers?"

"What?"

"He said, *Everybody has some story they don't need to tell.* And that was that."

I knew then from the way her voice sounded that she couldn't explain what she was feeling, or stop it. I didn't say anything then. I just sat at the table, watching her face.

"He and I haven't even screwed yet. If that's all it was, I wouldn't be doing it. I wouldn't put myself in this position. I wouldn't put Ray in it."

I didn't say anything, but I nodded.

"I can't tell you anything else, Vangie. I don't want to jinx it."

We did not have any more drinks after that, because Ray was due home at eleven, and because she had wanted the talk more than anything, not Jim Beam at all. And when I was leaving, because I didn't know what else to say, I said, "Well, I'm around."

"We didn't even talk about you."

I said, "It'll keep."

Even if we'd gone on talking that night, I wouldn't have told her what I'd done with Del's brother. She probably would have understood — certainly she would have understood now, if not before — but I did not want her to know. When I fucked Frank, I got a brand and a mark and a knowledge, but I did not want to go on fucking him. The brand was enough. It was my scar, the sign of an accident or an illness or an adventure gone wrong.

June didn't want a scar. She wasn't going to fuck Luke just for the feeling of it. She did not want to do the thing once and then keep it secret inside her. She wanted to go on living it. I did not know how a person could do that, if it could be done. But I guessed it could be done, because there she was living in the house with the two of them and talking about love. Love.

When I went out to my truck that night, I walked by Luke's pickup, and that's how I knew he hadn't gone into town. I figured he was probably up on the mountain — or maybe just out behind the house, waiting for me to leave. When I saw his truck, it made me think about the way men held themselves and the way they talked and moved, and I knew it was a foreign world June was in. After I moved in with Del, I felt like I was in a foreign land as well, but it had to be even more true for June, living out there with the two of them. But June was probably like smoke finding her way about that world, because she was nothing if not smart, and smoke always finds a way in and out.

I didn't say *shouldn't* or *can't* to her. Maybe as a friend I should have, but to me, whatever was happening between her and Luke, between her and Ray, had already started. She was in the current of it.

1 0

A F T E R Del had been work-
ing awhile, he started hanging out with the guys he crewed
with at Traut's. They were all older — in their twenties and
thirties and forties — and I think they saw Del as a little
brother. They usually went out for a beer after work, and for
some, the thing turned into a binge that lasted the whole
evening. I worked night shift and didn't get home until midnight or one, so it didn't really affect the time I had to spend
with Del, but I did know what was going on. A lot of
nights, he and I got home around the same time — me from
work and him from the bars. I listened to his drunken stories

as we ate a late meal, and then we showered, screwed, and slept. Or, in my case, lay waiting for sleep.

Along with all the other wives and girlfriends, at times I got invited to the crew parties. While I came to know the other women, I never really became friends with any of them. I don't know why. Maybe it was the difference in ages, maybe it was something else, but I never really let loose around those people. That made the other women think I was a snob, when all I really felt was shy. I did become kind of friendly with one woman, named Vicki, the wife of a guy named Len. She was in her late twenties and she was unlike anyone I had ever seen around Mahanaqua. She had this different way of dressing, and she gave me an idea of what I wanted to look like when I got older. The main thing about her look was she wore jackets — blazers, I guess you'd call them — with no shirt under them. The blazers looked normal at first, but when Vicki moved her hand to sweep back her hair or reach for a glass, the neckline shifted and plunged. The look showed off her chest and her lace bras and the pretty gold chains she wore. I figured when I got a few years older, I'd put away my tight jeans and lace-up shirts and go for Vicki's look.

Del knew how shy I felt around those women, but he still could not understand why I couldn't get along with them. The night of one particular kegger, I told him, "Go and have a good time without me."

"Come on. Vicki is going to be there. You can talk to her and get deep."

That made me laugh, because that's how Del described

any conversation I had with a woman, yet he was right, too, because when Vicki and I got talking, it was about when we got our first periods, and how Vicki got together with her husband, and all that kind of thing. For as good a time as I had talking to Vicki, though, it was never like talking to June, and all those "deep" conversations made me miss my friend.

"All right, I'll go," I said. "But I don't want to stay long."

"We'll leave whenever you want."

Of course Del headed off to the keg as soon as we got to the party, and I looked around for Vicki. It turned out she wasn't there, and I got stuck standing on the edges of a lot of conversations, smoking and nursing my beer. I did that for about an hour and a half, but then I couldn't take any more conversations about kids and who was getting divorced, and I went looking for Del. I felt like a dog sniffing for its owner.

He was drinking shots of Southern Comfort there at the keg. When I came near, I heard one of his friends, a guy named Kutz, say, "Here comes your woman, Pardee. Drink up."

When I got up to the keg, Kutz said to me, "What, don't you drink?"

"I drink."

"You look stone-cold sober to me."

"I'm fine."

"You ought to loosen up. Good-looking woman like you ought to have a good time."

"I'm having a good time. I have to work tomorrow."

"Hell, you'll be working your whole life! You don't see that stopping us, do you?"

I saw Del stick one finger in the air at Kutz, and as soon as I saw that, I knew Del was drunk. He speechified a lot when he was drunk, and a lot of times it started with a finger pointed in the air.

"Kutz," he said. "My woman's the hardest-working bitch you'll ever meet."

I let that one wash over me for a few seconds, and then I turned to Del and said, "Come get me when you're ready." And I went back to where some of the women were, and I sat down on the edge of a conversation and I made myself listen and smile.

In a little while Del came over and handed me his keys, and I took the both of us home.

I knew Del had to be a different kind of person at work, too. I knew he had to act tough, and I also think he had to act crazy because he was the young one. But I couldn't believe he would use a word like that to talk about me.

I never told him I was hurt. I probably should have, but I didn't want him to know. If he could hurt me with words, it meant the smallest things could injure me, and I didn't want to be that vulnerable, not even with him.

I pretended everything was normal between Del and me, and in a little while, it was. Three weekends later, though, when there was going to be a party at Laban Wolfe's house, I told Del I wasn't going. He thought I was bullshitting, though, because around nine he said, "Come on, I want to be leaving soon."

"I told you I didn't want to go."

"You'll go," he said, smiling. "Smoke a joint and you'll be fine."

"No, I deal with rude people all day. I don't need to deal with them at night."

Del looked at me for a long second after I said that, but he didn't say anything. He stood there in the living room, watching me, and at first I did not want to meet his eyes, but then I thought, why shouldn't I meet his eyes? I thought about the way he headed for the keg as soon as he got to a party, and the way I got ditched off to spend time with the "girls" — and of course that line of thinking led me right back to bitch night. I just didn't want to have anything to do with it.

"Go have fun by yourself," I said, looking straight at him. "Leave your dog at home."

I gave him credit. He waited awhile, trying to figure out my words, and when he couldn't, he gave up.

"Suit yourself," he said, and he walked out the back door.

THAT NIGHT when Del came home, he laid into me. I don't mean he hit me — I mean he laid me open. We fucked in about four positions, and he slammed into me in each one. He didn't talk at all, just pulled at my hips when he wanted me to move. In the end I was on top so he could have my breasts in his mouth and hands, and I was working hard to make him come so it all could stop. Then — and the two things happened almost together — he slapped me hard on my ass, and squeezed and bit my right breast so hard I thought he'd gone through skin.

The slap surprised me more than it hurt, but my breast felt like a knife had gone through it. I cried out. And I don't know if he thought it was a sound of pleasure or what, but a little bit after that he came.

When I climbed off him, I said, "Jesus Christ, Del, that hurt."

"Sorry," he said, but I heard the way he said it and knew from his voice he was still drunk. I didn't say anything else.

After he rolled onto his side, I waited until I heard his breathing change, and then I slipped out of the bed and went to the bathroom. When I checked my breast, I could see a bunch of the little specks of blood just under the skin from the last bite. The skin looked bubbly, like it was blistered, and blood was gathering in the blistered places. Even though no skin was broken, my breast felt like it was on fire.

I went downstairs to the kitchen, filled a plastic bag with ice from the freezer, and brought it back up to the bedroom. I lay with the ice on me, and even though I still did not sleep easily or well beside Del, I made myself sleep that night because I could not stand to be awake.

IN THE morning when the alarm rang, Del said, "What the hell?"

I opened my eyes and saw him touching a place on the bed with his hand.

"What is this from?" Del said as he touched the wet spot on the bed.

"I slept with an ice pack. I guess it melted."

"What, are you sick?"

"Maybe you could lighten up," I said, and I turned in the bed so he could see my breasts. The last place where he bit was even a darker purple-black than before. The black blood that filled the blistery places looked thick under the skin.

"I don't care if you slap me on the ass, but this is too much," I said. I watched him, but I didn't know what I saw in his face when he looked at my body. "You were so drunk you probably don't even remember doing it."

"I remember it, Vangie," he said, but by then I had turned away from him in the bed.

I did not get up to make him breakfast or pack his lunch. I didn't do anything for him. Before he left for work, he came back upstairs and stood in the doorway of our room.

"I'm sorry," he said from the doorway.

I did not open my eyes.

"Vangie, it'll never happen again."

I heard him move into the room then, and I figured he was going to try to kiss me or some shit, but then I heard him move away and go back down the stairs. When I did open my eyes, I saw why he'd come back into the room: he'd made me another bag of ice, wrapped it in a towel, and left it on the edge of the bed.

11

I wanted to talk to June, but when I called out to the house, the telephone rang and rang. I figured she was with Luke, so I didn't try to go out there. While part of me wanted to talk to her about Del and about what was going on, I also didn't want her to know. I wouldn't know how to launch into all the things I had on my mind — I couldn't even picture myself really saying the words. So I stayed away.

That week Del and I did not talk about what had happened, but he was on his best behavior. He bought me new wiper blades for my truck and changed the oil, he put a hook on the screen door that I'd been wanting ever since we moved in, and he brushed out my hair every night when I came home from Dreisbach's stinking from grease and sweat. He was so well behaved that it was hard to even act natural with him, and I felt self-conscious and quiet. After a while, things mostly went back to the way they were before, but there was still a little place in me that was walled off from Del. I knew it would be that way for a while. Even though I could not stand having hurt feelings or being so self-conscious, I couldn't change everything I felt.

I worked the next Friday night, and a little after eleven, I saw Del waiting for me there in the hallway of Dreisbach's, next to the bread rack.

"I came to see if you'd go out with me," he said, and just the way he said the words, I knew he'd already had a drink or two.

"I don't think so. I'm supposed to work until midnight."

"It's not what you think," he said. "I won't drink anymore if you don't want me to."

I stood looking at him a long time. He never showed up at my work like that, and I guess it touched me. Something must have showed in my face, because he took my hands and pulled them up to his chest. When he kissed me, it was exactly the kind of kiss I liked best: a little hard, a little biting, but also soft.

"Go see if you can get off early," he said.

For whatever reason, Earl decided to be nice to me, or maybe he took one look at Del — who came to stand just outside the kitchen doorway — and thought it had to be something pressing if he was showing up for me like that.

"You serve this burger, you can go," he said.

When I left, the last customer was eating in near darkness, because Earl had turned out nearly all the lights in the dining room. Out in the parking lot, Del made me leave my truck there and ride with him.

"Where to?" I said.

"The Ruby. Want to?"

"I'm ready."

As soon as we got in his car, Del slipped his hand between my legs and I let him. We hadn't had sex all week, and I knew Del was wondering if later I'd let him slip in that way, too. Part of me was still thinking about the bruises, and another part of me couldn't wait to push it all away from me. I could feel myself getting the shivery feeling with just his hand outside my pantyhose and underwear.

We still weren't legal, but the Ruby would serve anyone who could reach the bar. There were a good number of people in the place when we got there, but it was not as exciting as it seemed the times I'd been there before to buy packages to take out. No one was playing the jukebox, no one was playing mini-bowling or darts. People were just drinking and talking. Del and I sat down at one of the tables, and even though no one was looking at us, I felt self-conscious about being there in my waitress uniform. At least it was a black one, and not all white like I sometimes wore.

"I wish you would have told me at home we were coming here," I said. "I would have brought clothes."

"Would you have come if I asked?"

"I don't know. Maybe."

"Maybe," Del said. "You hardly talked to me all week."

"Do you blame me?"

He squirreled around in his pocket until he came up with four quarters.

"Go pick some songs." He waited a second before he handed them over to me. "I don't blame you," he said.

"You want to help me pick?"

"Naw, you go ahead." He moved his head in the direction of the bar. "What should I get you?"

"A screwdriver."

It took me a while to find ten songs I liked on that juke-box. By the time I got back to the table and the drink Del had waiting for me, one of his cronies from Traut's was parked at one of our extra chairs. I sat down, and though Del slipped his hand over my nyloned knee as soon as I pulled in my chair, he did not stop his talking or introduce me to the guy sitting with us.

The guy was talking to Del about hunting. Buck season was about to open, and all of Traut's had the day off from work for the opener. Like most places in Mahanaqua, including the schools, Traut's closed down for the first day of buck season because it wouldn't have paid to run the factory with so many guys taking vacation or calling in sick. The guy Del was talking to had his stand all built, his area staked out, and he could not believe Del's plans to kill a deer were not as elaborate as his own.

"I'll probably just go on out with my dad and brother," Del said.

What the guy couldn't know, what Del didn't say, was

that Del didn't hunt anymore. Not at all. He'd started hunting when he was ten, he got his first buck when he was
twelve, and he puked when he had to skin that dead buck.
After, his father beat him for getting sick over it. I was the
only one who knew that story — along with his brother
Frank and his old man, who liked to use his fists so much to
decorate his boys' faces.

But I did not say anything as I sat and listened. After a
long time, the guy finally seemed to understand that while
Del might go strolling out in the woods with a gun over his
shoulder, he had no real plans on how to kill a deer, or how
to get the buck with the biggest rack, or anything like that.

"So you don't want to try to get yourself a ten-point
buck?" the guy said.

"I got one already," Del said. "She's my ten-point buck."

For the first time in the conversation the guy had to look
over at me. Del took his hand from my thigh and slipped it
around my back, touching my shoulder blades through my
uniform. The guy didn't stay too long after that.

After he walked away, I said to Del, "He doesn't know
what to make of you."

"What?"

"You just told him you like pussy better than hunting."

Del did not say anything, but he narrowed his eyes, studying me.

"What if I do?" he said after a while.

"I guess it would be a first in this town."

When we got home, the night was all about me. I knew
it was still part of the be-nice-to-Vangie campaign, but I

didn't care. Del was careful in how he touched me — cupping my breasts only and not kneading them, kissing them but not sucking. He did not try to get inside me, just used his fingers and his tongue until he made me come. He was going to do it a second time, but I stopped his hand.

"What's wrong?"

"Nothing," I told him. "I'm just resting."

We lay there, his hand brushing back and forth over my hip. It was peaceful in the darkness.

"What are you thinking about?" I said.

"I'm thinking how smooth your skin is."

When he said it, I wondered how he had learned to do that, to say exactly the right thing. I wondered if it was a thing all pretty boys just knew how to do.

I climbed on top of him then, but when he went to touch me, I took his hands in mine and moved them above his head, pinning them against the mattress. He struggled against my weight for a second, and then he understood what I was doing, and he let me hold him down. I kissed him and I moved my body over his body, but I did not let him touch me with his hands.

I had just gotten him up inside me, and had my nipple — on my good breast, not the one where he'd almost bitten through the skin — in his mouth when I started talking to him.

"Am I your ten-point buck?"

"What?"

"Am I your ten-point buck," I said.

"You know you are."

"Not a doe?"

"Not a doe."

"All right," I said. "I'll be a buck. But don't you forget."

"What, honey?"

"I let you catch me."

"So you did," he said. "So you did."

We fucked then, me rocking on him and stopping, rocking and stopping. We did it a long time, and I kept feeling like I was dripping down around him. I'd never felt that wet before just from screwing, and I couldn't get enough of the feeling. It was not like coming, but something in me just kept opening and opening.

After a time, Del couldn't take it anymore. I let him move his hands, and he wrapped his arms around my back so he could fuck hard up into me. There were no more words then, no more talk, but I'd already heard everything I wanted to hear.

My ten-point buck — to anyone else, it probably would have sounded stupid, calling a woman a deer. But I'd seen Del's face there in the Ruby when he said it the first time, and I had his cock up inside me when I made him say it again. I never forgot the bruises, but I never forgot those words, either.

1 2

THE following weekend, June
called. She asked how I was, but by that time things had settled down between Del and me. My bruises were two weeks
old and almost gone, and it seemed pointless to go into the
whole thing. I figured she had enough on her plate. "I've
been better, but I've been worse," I told her. "How's the
love nest?"

"Be serious, Vangie. I need to talk to you."

"I'm listening," I said.

She told me they'd gone out shining deer, she and Luke
and Ray. She didn't like the way they used the lights against
the deer, but she was glad she went anyway.

"I wanted to sit between the two of them," she said. "I wanted to know what it felt like."

And of course it wasn't the leg of the one who already was her lover that she concentrated on when it pressed against hers, and it wasn't his warmth she missed when he got out of the truck to check a stand.

When they got back to the house, she stayed out on the porch to smoke, because she didn't want to go in the house, not yet, not for another night. Luke came out to find her, and they stood smoking in the dark air while Ray was inside.

June said they didn't talk at all. She said she heard Luke move before she felt his touch. Then his hand was there, reaching under her hair to the nape of her neck.

"His fingers were so cool and smooth, Vangie," she said.

She told me she was sure then that Luke had to know her in a way no one else knew her, because that was her favorite place to be touched — her neck and her face and her hair — and Ray never touched her there.

"Do you know what I'm saying?"

"I know," I said, and it was a lie and it was the truth. I knew what it meant to be touched in a way you liked, but I didn't know what it meant to June to be touched by Luke. There was no way for me to know.

She told me she and Luke had sex for the first time the next morning, after Ray left for work. She went to Luke's room, and they fucked in Luke's bed. She said it wasn't like anything she ever did.

That was all she told me. It wasn't like when we were in high school and we recounted every detail.

"Say something," she said at the end.

"I'm glad you found someone. I'm glad you love him."

"But?"

"But nothing. Just be careful."

She laughed at that. "You mean if I can't be good, be careful?"

"Yeah, something like that."

"I'll call when I can," she said. "When I have something new to tell."

But I didn't hear from her again for a long time.

13

D E L and I crossed some kind
of line the night he called me a buck. Maybe it had to do
with me trusting him again, or maybe it had to do with me
pinning him to the mattress. I didn't know. What I was sure
of was that our sex changed.

If it had happened earlier, I might have been scared,
because I wouldn't have known how to want the things we
began to do. And maybe I should have been frightened that
Del wanted to take so much from my body, because of the
bruising and all. But I was not frightened. I wanted everything we did.

It started with talk, with words. One night I came home

from Dreisbach's and found that — surprise of surprises — Del had gotten home before me and had actually gone to bed. I snuck around the house in the dark, showering, combing out my hair, and Del didn't call out to me during any of it.

I thought for sure when I climbed into bed he was going to tell me he was sick, but when I slipped beside him and wrapped myself around his back, he said, "Do you want some of my cock?"

I was still damp from my shower, and it felt good to take him in my arms, he was so dry and warm. I could smell that he'd been smoking weed, but I didn't care — when he got stoned he was never rough, and he could fuck for a long time. I kissed his shoulder blades and shoulders, then I reached over his arm to his belly and down to his cock, which was hard and warm.

"I want this," I said.

"How do you want me to fuck you?"

"I want to be able to kiss you."

"Do you want me to eat your pussy?"

"You know I do."

"Ask for it then, because you know I will if you ask."

"Do I have to ask?"

"I like to hear you say it."

"Then Del, will you eat my pussy?"

He moved away from me in the bed, away from my hand holding his cock, and turned on the light.

"Could you kneel, Vangie? I want to see it."

So I got on my hands and knees, and he knelt behind me.

"You know how you look right now? You look all fat and wet. Is that what you want me to eat?"

"That's what I want you to eat."

So he did. He ate me, fingered me, and he fucked me. I didn't know if I was going to feel his tongue or his fingers or his cock.

It got to be a game between us, that position. Sometimes Del would have me kneel but leave my panties on. He'd tease me by kissing me through the fabric or pulling the sides of the crotch enough aside to kiss my skin — but not far enough to kiss my wetness. When he did finally take my panties down, he'd do it slow, inch by inch, kissing me as he went. And he'd tease me about how wet I was.

"If I put my finger inside you and you're wet, you know what you're going to have to do."

I'd ask what, and each time it was different. Sometimes he told me he was going to have to spank me. He'd hit me with his hand hard enough to hurt, but not too hard. Other times he'd tell me I had to suck his balls. Once he said something to me, and it took me a while to even put the words together.

"If your pussy's wet, you're going to have to swallow my fuck," he said, and for some reason, those words stayed on my mind for a long time after.

In that position, it was also just a hop and a skip and a jump to fucking me in the ass, and Del learned to do that so it never hurt. He'd use his tongue first, then get out the K-Y jelly and use his fingers.

One night, after he was all the way in, I told him, "My pussy gets lonely when we do it like this."

"We need to get you a dildo so I can treat your pussy right."

"Naw, I just want you," I said.

But when he brought a dildo home — a bright orange one that looked clowny to me — I let him use it. It all felt so good, being full up in *there,* and being full up in *there.* Though I never felt this way at night, when I saw the stuff beside the bed in the morning — the pink-orange dildo that was the color of no one's skin, the crimped-up tube of jelly, the black cock ring that we were just starting to use — I felt embarrassed and kind of sickened. Other times seeing our toys made me feel like a woman, like Del and I had secrets that no one at Dreisbach's or in Mennonite Town or in all of Mahanaqua could guess at.

I think Del was embarrassed about the dildo, too, but not in the same way I was. He just never wanted to wash the thing. He wanted it to be there magically on our nightstand, and he wanted to be able to put it anywhere in me — but he didn't want to know too many details.

"You don't want me to get an infection, do you?" I said when he asked me why I was wiping the thing down with alcohol the first time.

"What are you talking about?"

So we had to have a talk about how he couldn't go from my ass to my pussy, not with a dildo and not with his cock, and he got kind of pissed about the whole thing. He wanted to do whatever he liked in any sequence he liked.

"Why do you have to make it so complicated?"

"I'm just telling you what I read," I said.

So I was in charge of cleanup, and I was the one who had

to say no and scoot away sometimes. Sometimes Del did the stuff anyway, and I'd spend the next couple days smelling myself, trying to see if my odor changed the way my pamphlet from the Ontelaunee clinic said it would if I had an infection. But my smell never changed, and I was not always sorry when Del crossed over my lines. If I was all caught up in what we were doing, it was hard for me to say no. Sometimes I wanted him to go on touching me and touching me, playing in my pussy and my ass, and I did not say no to anything. I wanted what I wanted, too.

I SAW more of June's brother than I did of June those days. Kevin wasn't exactly a regular, but when he did come in to the restaurant, he always sat at my tables, he always asked me how I was, and he always gave me a compliment. It was the same kind of flirting everyone did with me, but over time I got to be more and more aware of Kevin. I was aware of him not only as a result of the stories about him, but also for the way he seemed to live within the stories that were told.

One night, right after I got bitched at by Earl — because instead of just slapping salad into a bowl, I'd actually taken five extra seconds to arrange the tomato like a flower, which Earl thought was a waste of time — Kevin seemed to know things were rough.

"He should be glad you work here," he told me. "You're the best thing about this place."

It was nice to hear the words after just getting screamed at, and I wanted to be nice to him back. So I said, "The best thing, huh? Well, where have you been all my life?"

"In prison."

At first it felt like a bomb had dropped, but then I realized that was why Kevin said it. It wasn't like people didn't already have it on their minds as soon as they saw him, so it was his to joke about if he wanted.

I said, "Was the food any better there?"

He didn't say anything to that, but he smiled, and I knew I had been right to say it.

That comment sort of broke the ice, and I came to see him as a kind of friend. If I had the time, I would sometimes grab a cup of coffee and sit with Kevin at his table. The only other person I felt safe doing that with was Bill Mahlon, because he was older than my dad. But I felt safe doing it with Kevin, too, in spite of everything, because he was June's brother and because I felt that I knew the worst there was to know about him. In a way, that made me like him, because there was no secret about him. I still was scared of him, but I knew that people could be more than one thing at a time. I didn't think what he let happen to June when she was ten was right, but he was also the person who had been tender with her when she was eight, driving her around until she got dizzy watching the sky. He committed a crime, but he'd served time for it. He was what he was.

Kevin and I never talked about anything important anyway. Work and the weather. But kind people who peppered my day were a type of friend, and their compliments, or their teasing, or just the sight of their faces, meant something to me. No matter how busy we got, even if I overlooked him for a bit, Bill Mahlon was always patient and called me the Peekaboo Girl and made sure I got my dollar tip. The game warden who teased me about the time he caught me and June skipping school and swimming out at Sweet Arrow Lake always made sure I got a dollar tip from each of the guys at his table. Kevin Keel always said I was pretty in whatever color I had on that day and made sure I got my tip. I didn't give a shit if the reason they gave me money was because they could see the flowers on my underwear or not. Because as tough as I pretended to be, I still craved kindness, and I took it where I could find it.

14

One night around quarter to ten the phone rang. Before I even answered, I knew it was June. When I picked up the receiver, though, I heard a lot of noise and crackling, and I thought, no, it's Del calling from a bar, wanting me to come pick him up.

"Hey, it's me," June said.

"Where are you?"

"Eighty-one. At the rest stop."

"What are you doing there?"

June said, "Oh, it's a long story. I'll tell you sometime. I just called to ask a favor."

One of the rigs picked that moment to pull on through. When the roaring was done, I said, "What's the favor?"

"If Ray calls, tell him I just left. Tell him I just left your place. I told him I was running out to see you."

"What for?" I said.

"Please, Vangie. I don't think he'll call, but help me out just this once."

"No, I mean, what did you tell him you were coming out here for? What's the story?"

"I said you needed help hemming a couple uniforms. I couldn't think of anything else."

I said, "If I hem them much shorter, I might as well not wear a skirt at all." Another rig pulled out then, and after the sound passed I said, "What are you doing up there anyway?"

"Getting cleaned up. I couldn't go home like I was."

"Where were you before now?"

"In the woods."

And it took me that long into the conversation to understand what the situation was and what June was asking. She and Luke weren't just screwing in the house when Ray was at work — she'd left Ray at home, waiting, so she could go fuck Luke in the woods, and she wanted to use me as a cover.

"Jesus Christ, June," I said. "Don't you think that's dangerous?"

"No one saw us. I'll tell you more later."

"Okay, okay," I said. "Are you going home now?"

"Straight home from here."

"Where's Luke?"

"I don't know. He'll wait a couple hours before he goes back. He's probably in a bar."

"So you're there by yourself?"

"I have to go, Vangie. I'll tell you more later."

"All right. I got it," I said, and she hung up.

After I hung up, I sat there in my kitchen in Mennonite Town, picturing June washing up at the rest stop on the interstate. I knew the place. There was a line of sinks — one of them with a tall, curved faucet where you could wash your hair if you needed to. I pictured June standing in a stall, washing with wet fingers and paper towels.

It was crazy what June was doing, and I was crazy myself for being part of it. I wasn't doing a goddamn thing wrong, and yet here I was, caught up in a lie and worrying a liar's worry over it. It was bad enough each time I didn't tell Del the truth about what was happening to Ray, but I didn't also want to be June's alibi. To withhold information was one thing — I withheld information from Del every single day of my life when I didn't tell him about Frank — but I did not want to have to tell a lie. I did not want to put my mouth around the words.

As it turned out, all my worrying was for nothing. Ray didn't call that night or any other night, and that was the only time I ever got a phone call like that from June. Either she and Luke planned their outings better, or June took it on faith that I'd invent a story if I had to. That's how much she trusted me, but that's also how well she knew me. Because while I could resolve not to lie when I was sitting by myself in my house, when the time came I'd probably do what came most naturally. I knew myself well enough to say that. And June knew me that well, too.

THAT FRIDAY I came home early from dinner shift one night because I was feeling so bad. I stayed long enough to help Lorraine serve the "mad rush" of the dinner crowd and barely made it through, and I was sure I had some kind of fever, because nothing else would make me feel so stupid and weak. The whole drive home, I kept to forty. When I pulled up to the house, I was surprised to see Del's car. When he worked the seven-to-three shift, he usually went out partying with his buddies. I was glad, though, because I figured all I had to do was make it into the house and he'd be able to take care of me if I did have the flu. When I walked in the house, though, I found Del sitting at the kitchen table, high from sniffing a can of PAM.

I couldn't even believe it. He'd sprayed PAM into a bag and inhaled the fumes — there among the breakfast dishes and crumbs, there beside the refrigerator and stove. He still had the bag in his hand when I walked in the door. When he turned to look at me, his eyes were so far gone I knew he was high, high, high.

"Vangie, get me a washcloth, just a washcloth," was the only thing he said. I guessed he wanted to wash the grease off his face from where he had been holding the bag to his nose and mouth. He looked at me a little while, and then put his head down on the table.

I took the bag from his hand, threw it in the trash, and then just stood and watched him. I'd never seen anyone huff before. It was something I'd only ever heard of, read about. It must have been a gentle kind of high, because Del's hand had no tension in it when I took the greasy plastic from him.

In a couple seconds, he looked up at me again and said, "Vangie, a washcloth."

I ran the water until it got hot. I soaked a washcloth and smeared soap on part of it. I ended up washing his face for him, still there in the kitchen, him sitting on a chair, me standing between his legs.

When I was done, I said, "I'm going to bed. I'm sick."

"Okay," he said. "Okay. I'll be up later."

"I threw out the can and the bag," I said.

"That's all right," he said.

When he came to bed later, I felt sick — as much from what Del looked like sitting in that kitchen chair as from whatever bug was in my body. I didn't really want to touch him, but when he started moving up against me, I knew he wouldn't sleep without sex. So I let him fuck me. Or I let someone fuck me — I didn't know who. He didn't talk to me at all, and he didn't touch me — except to stick his penis into me. After, he slid away and fell asleep. I thought of going downstairs to sleep on the sofa, but I felt weak and hot and didn't want to move. I didn't know what difference it would have made at that point, anyway. If I let him fuck me, it didn't seem like I should care about sleeping beside his body.

DEL TOLD me he huffed the PAM because he didn't want to drink and we didn't have any weed.

"I didn't know you'd be home so soon, Vangie. I heard about it, and I wanted to try it."

"Yeah, well I heard about it, too," I said. "But I hear a lot of things I'd never do."

"It was a onetime thing. I didn't want to drink. I didn't want to hurt you."

"Don't you think it's a pretty funny way not to hurt me? Sniffing PAM?"

"I guess. I don't know."

That was how he worked it out in his mind: he bruised and bit me when he was drunk, so if he didn't get drunk again, he knew he couldn't do the same thing. Smoking dope didn't fall into the same category, and neither did huffing.

I had to hand it to him. That was the idea he stuck to: he was not going to hurt me again as a result of alcohol. But because he could not or would not stop getting drunk, by the next weekend he had to add a new element to his plan: if he did decide to drink, he had to stay away from me completely. So he didn't come home Friday after work, and I didn't get a call from him. Nothing. He just disappeared. All that night I kept waiting to hear him come up the stairs and say, "Vangie," but he didn't. Part of me was scared he would never come back, and part of me was mad that he would.

On Saturday when I heard him come in, I was lying in our bed, listening to a cardinal call, over and over. I was lying on my side in the bed, facing the doorway, and I didn't move when Del came to the doorway of the room. I let him look at me a long time, and I let myself look at him a long time.

He said, "You look surprised to see me."

I didn't say anything.

"Don't ever think I'm not coming back, Vangie."

"No?"

"No. Don't ever think that."

"I can't promise what I'll think," I said.

"Well, don't think I'm not coming back."

"All I think is I don't know you anymore," I said. "That's all." I turned away from him then.

He could still see my back, though, and he could read that just like he could read any other part of me, so in a little while he said, "You know me, Vangie. No one knows me better than you."

I did not say anything but went on listening to the cardinal's call.

"Can I come lay with you?"

When I didn't answer, he said, "Vangie, please. Can I come lay down with you?"

"I don't care," I told him. "It's your bed, too."

When he got into bed with me, I did not turn to kiss him and I did not move my hand over his hand when he put his arm over my belly. I lay there, and I let him lie at my back. That was all. In the end, though, it was the same as taking him back into my heart. A short trip through muscle and bone.

15

WHEN Del started staying away one or two nights a week, I had lots of time alone. Because I did not want to think about Del, I made myself think about other things and other people. Sometimes I thought of my mom, who had sent me a picture of her and her ex-Mormon. Even though my mom was smiling in the picture and wearing a turquoise ring on almost every finger, the picture worried me. I thought the ex-Mormon looked skinny and mean, and it made me sad to think of my mom being with him. It didn't make me feel much better to think of June, but those nights when Del was gone, I mostly ended up thinking of her out there in that house with Luke and Ray.

I thought I understood some of June's motivation. She wanted to be loved, and she wanted to be the center of attention. But I wondered what it meant to her to sleep with two brothers. What did it serve in her? Maybe she wanted cock from one brother who was full and thick in her arms and one who was thin enough to have the face of a hawk. Or maybe she really could talk to Luke. Maybe a hundred things. I knew enough about June to understand that the key for her was *brothers,* but there had to be something she needed from each and something she got from each. As for Luke — well, I knew from Del how two brothers could grow up together and keep hate in a trundle bed between them, pulling it out when it was needed, when there was no one else to hate.

It all made me think of the stories I heard about Kevin Keel. Everyone knew the who-what-where-when of Kevin Keel, but they never knew the why. Why did he become what he was? Nobody could tell me that story, just like they couldn't tell me why he stayed in a place where everyone knew him as a hell-raiser, a user, and a killer. Maybe he did not know how to be anything else, and it served his fear to stay, or maybe he figured that whatever his story was, it was his, and he might as well stay no matter what people thought of him.

All I knew for certain was that none of us did anything for long unless we wanted to. June and Luke wanted the lies and danger and hurtfulness, at least in part. They might not have known they wanted those things, but something pulled them to that water and they did not draw back.

I pictured the two of them in my mind like they were in a movie, and I ran the movie over and over in my head those nights I was alone. I pictured June waiting until Ray's car pulled away in the morning, and then crossing the hall soundlessly to stand beside Luke's bed. He was the first one to speak.

Why so quiet? He's long gone.

Aren't you afraid, ever?

Of him? No, I'm not afraid of him.

Are you afraid of me? That I'll get tired of it?

Never. You're here because you want to be.

They'd kiss, and sometimes she'd steal just that much and hurry on in to work. Other times she'd have to move the sheets back from Luke's body so she could see. His narrow hips and cock would be so pretty they'd make something ache inside her, and she'd have to bend to kiss his hipbones and the small paths of veins running down to his cock. Those mornings she would not go to work at all, but it didn't matter — they were always looking for women to pay minimum wage to, and what was a job anyway, except a way to keep food on the table. What she did with Luke was the only living.

Did he give it to you last night?

You know he did. You heard it.

Then what do you want from me?

This. And this. Everything.

I knew they were my words and my fucking — because I couldn't know what it was like between them. But I wanted to picture them so I could understand, so I could feel close. So I could have something to think about other than my own life in that house with Del. If what passed between June and Luke all happened a different way, different from the one I imagined, then it did, and my picturing did no good. Did no good.

16

O N E Friday at the end of
June, Del disappeared again, but he did not come home at
the end of the weekend, he did not come home on Monday, and he did not come home on Tuesday or Wednesday
or Thursday. On the seventh day running, I couldn't stand it
anymore, so about ten o'clock at night, I took one of my tip
dimes and called Del's job from the pay phone at Dreisbach's. When I talked to the supervisor, I found out that
he'd made it in to Traut's to work all of his shifts that week.
That meant that the only place he wasn't making it was
home to me.

When I found that out, something inside me just broke.

I usually liked the late part of my shift because I had a little time to myself. I could pee, play a song or two on the jukebox, think my own thoughts. Some nights I'd bring a cup of coffee to a back booth so I could sit down and fold napkins. After working on my feet all day, it was sweet just to sit down for a while. But that night I did none of those things. I did not want to sit at a back booth folding napkins, and I did not want to think my own thoughts.

When I saw Kevin Keel at one of my tables, I knew he would help me pass the time. I thought that if I could just hear a friendly voice in that dining room, I'd be all right. So I took his order for a rib eye steak and I got him a Yuengling from the bar and I talked about anything and nothing, just to fill up the air. I told him how ungodly hot it was getting in the back room where we had to do our dishes, now that the weather was turning. I told him how I spilled water that night when I was serving my old high school principal and his wife. I told him how you could always tell it was Friday night, because the farmers came in wearing black dress shoes with their overalls and white socks. Kevin was kind and listened to me fill up the air with all of that.

He was finishing his dessert when I went up to his table with his green guest check. I believe he thought I was going to sit down and tell him some more about my vision of the world and the dinner crowd, but I didn't.

"I'm going to play you a song on the jukebox," I said instead. "Is that all right with you?"

"Sure it's all right. Are you going to sit with me and listen?"

"No, I'm going to do dishes. You listen and tell me if you like the song or not."

I took a quarter from my tip bowl, went to the jukebox, and punched in the numbers for "Would You Lay with Me (In a Field of Stone)" by Tanya Tucker. I didn't think twice about it. I did not know I was going to do it, yet something in me must have known, because I did the thing without thinking.

In the back room I did exactly one load of cups and glasses: I put the plastic tray in the dishwasher, let it cycle through, pulled cups and glasses out, put them lip down on the drying table. I felt bad then for some reason, panicky and sick that Kevin Keel was sitting out there listening to a song I played for him, but I thought, *You started it, Vangie, you finish it.*

Kevin was smoking a cigarette when I came up to his table. He had both arms up on the table, and I looked at the skin of his forearms and then through the smoke to his face.

"So that's what you played for me," he said.

"That's what I played."

"What's it mean?"

I said, "What do you think it means?"

"Says you want to lay down with me."

I looked at the little hollow place right at the base of his throat, the place where the skin curved in over the hollow. I thought how I would be able to touch Kevin where the skin pulled over his collarbone, and how I would put my mouth on the hard bone. I liked the words *lay down* and I liked hearing a man say them.

"Well then, that's what I mean."

"I thought you had an old man."

"I did. I do," I said, because I didn't know which one was true of Del anymore. "Does it bother you?"

"Don't bother me, but it ought to bother him."

Kevin sat a while longer, taking me in, then he said, "All right. How late are you working?"

I didn't think it would happen that night, but then I thought, why not? I didn't know what difference it made anymore, and I didn't want to be alone in that house again.

When I told him midnight, he said, "All right. I'll be back."

I told him I'd be ready. Because of course all the while there were currents flowing in other people, there was one flowing in me, too.

AFTER I finished shift, I washed my face and neck and as much of my chest and arms as I could get to with the soap in the globe dispenser in the ladies. After, I used the rough brown paper towels to dry. The grease from the kitchen clung to my hair and made it heavy and shiny, but I couldn't do anything about it, or my smell — cigarette smoke, french fries, sweat. I thought I was going to be a pretty smelly date, and I thought of telling Kevin I'd changed my mind, but then I remembered that I did not want to be alone, and I remembered the way Kevin looked at me after I played the song. I decided he wouldn't care if I reeked of Dreisbach's.

He was waiting in the side entry hall when I came out of the bathroom, and he smiled at me. I thought how I could see June's face someplace in his, and I tried not to feel so scared about what I was doing.

"Are you ready to go out now?"

"I'm ready," I said.

I wondered if anyone was there watching as we walked out the side door of Dreisbach's, but it seemed there was no one anywhere, just the stink of the trash cans and the whir of the kitchen fan.

"Been wanting to ask you out a long time, to tell you the truth," Kevin said, taking my hand.

"Why didn't you?"

"It seemed like you were happy."

I kept my hand loose in his. His hand felt funny to me, the skin and bones so different from Del's, but I was glad to be holding hands. I couldn't remember the last time Del and I had done that. Fuck, yes, but hold hands? That I couldn't recall.

"I was happy," I said. "I'm not now."

"I'm sorry to hear that," Kevin Keel said.

We did not talk much in his truck. I watched him drive, and again I wondered what I was doing. But I thought again of the house, and how, if I weren't with Kevin, I'd be alone there, waiting to hear Del's car pull up or hear him open the door. I thought anything was better than that.

Kevin took me to Sweet Arrow and parked in a place I'd never been before, there on the south side, down a dirt road I didn't know. He put on a tape and played it just on his battery.

"You like that?"

"I like it," I said.

"You like the lake?"

"Yeah, I like it."

He laughed at me. I was nervous, and he knew it. He lit a joint and passed it to me, and I took a heavy toke.

"Now you'll relax," Kevin told me. "You're thinking too hard."

"I'm always like that."

We sat in silence then, listening to the tape. I liked the music okay — Jackson Browne's "Running on Empty."

"You believe that? 'You gotta do what you can to keep your love alive'?"

"I don't know," I said. "I never thought about it."

I was trying to think of some way to answer the question when he passed his hand over my breasts. He did not turn to face me, he just stuck out the arm that was between us and passed his hand over the front of my uniform. He found each of my nipples, and he pulled at them through the fabric.

"Don't think so hard," he said. "It's just a song."

I knew then that I didn't want him to touch me, but I didn't stop him. I let him go on feeling me sideways, then I let him pull me up against him. He opened the zipper on my uniform and took my breasts in his hands, squeezing them through my bra.

"So, you need a good dicking down," Kevin said.

I knew then that whatever kind of fantasy I had cooked up in my mind wasn't going to come true. I made the movement to kiss him, because I thought if we could kiss, if we could at least have good kisses between us, maybe it would be all right.

His kisses were dull and wet, and the taste of his mouth sickened me. But by then I did not know how to stop. He had taken off my bra, and my uniform was down around my waist. It seemed easiest to go through with it then, since I was the one who started it. I still did not know — it was not clear in my mind — that I should have done anything to get away from him: get down on my hands and knees, crawl naked through the woods.

Kevin Keel started by eating me, but what he did was more like ripping. Maybe that was when my skin began to tear — later I wasn't sure. What I did know was that after he got done snarling into my cunt, he fucked me so hard I thought I could feel my skin pulling and breaking. I was so scared I wasn't wet at all except from his spit. I tried not to move, tried to let him up my dry cunt.

He pumped into me awhile, then he said, "Good pussy doesn't just lie there."

So I pushed back against him and made noise. I thought if he came, it could all be over.

Instead it lasted a long time. When I started to cry, he said, "Is it sore?"

"Yes," I said, but I would not look at him when I said it.

"I'm almost done," he told me.

At the end, as he came, he slapped my face once, hard. Then he jerked out of me.

"Nice set of tits," he said when he climbed off me.

I didn't say anything. I was shaking and had trouble

pulling on my clothes. I didn't even try to put my nylons back on, because of the burning between my legs.

Keel took me back into town, to Dreisbach's, where I was parked. When I went to get out of his truck, he pulled me to him and kissed me.

"Sweet dreams," he said after he wiped his mouth on my mouth.

I walked away without looking back. When I got into my truck, I couldn't believe everything in it looked just the way it had when I left it that afternoon: the box of tissues, the crumpled napkins, my sweater. I sat a long time with my arms wrapped over the steering wheel, but stuff started seeping out of me and it burned, and I thought I better get on home.

I stood a long time on the back porch of the house before I could go in. I didn't know why. Del still wasn't home and there was no one to see me, but I just couldn't bring myself to put my hand on the doorknob and turn it and go inside. But I made myself do it, just like I made myself wash between my legs, over and over, even though the soap burned and it hurt to pass the washcloth over myself. I washed my hair three times, not to cut through the grease of the kitchen like I usually did, but to get Keel's whispers out of my hair. When I was finished, I could not smell him, but there was nothing left of me, either.

I did two more things before I went to bed that night. I washed my blood out of the skirt of my uniform, because it was already turning dark. There was not a lot of blood, and it wasn't in blots like when my period began. This blood stained the fabric in thin, red streaks. Then I ran the water until it was icy cold, and I soaked a washcloth in it. I took that washcloth back to the bed with me, and I lay with it between my legs until the heat from my body warmed it. When I was lying there I knew for the first time that June had told me only half the truth about Kevin. It wasn't one of his friends who fucked her when she was ten — it was Kevin. It all fit. I didn't let myself think anything else about it.

For the first time in days, I hoped Del would not come home. I didn't hate him anymore. I just hoped he would stay away.

17

I needn't have worried about Del coming home. His mother called me the next morning to tell me he was in detox at the hospital in Deer Run. He had overdosed on alcohol and quaaludes, and had almost stopped breathing. The police had picked him up. As he wasn't allowed any phone calls from the hospital, she was calling.

"I don't approve of you two living together," she said. "But I know you care for him."

"I do care for him," I said.

"Did you know any of this was going on?"

"I knew he was drinking," I said. I didn't think there was any point in telling her about the huffing.

"He has a lot of lessons to learn," she said, and then she told me it was God's will he didn't die.

When I asked her what I could do, she told me I couldn't do anything. He wasn't allowed any visitors, not even her or his old man. She told me I could pray, and that she and Del's dad were praying. I didn't know how all the praying fit into the way Del's old man used to beat Del, but I didn't get into it on the phone.

And though I did not believe in any of it, I did pray for Del to be all right. I didn't pray for the one thing I really wanted — to take back everything that had happened with Kevin Keel. I knew I couldn't have it, so I didn't bother to ask for it.

BY THE next afternoon it hurt so much I could barely walk or pee. I took down the small mirror we had nailed to the bathroom wall, sat on the bed, and held the mirror between my legs. It took me only a few seconds to find the tears that burned. One was on the small lip leading up to my clitoris. The place was swollen with black blood. The other tear was right at the bottom of my clitoris. Keel had split the bottom of that round button. They were small rips, but they ached and burned when I moved or when my urine hit the open skin. Who knew what was torn inside my vagina where I couldn't see.

I took myself to the hospital in Ontelaunee. The nurse thought I was another VD patient and asked me to name my partners.

"He wasn't a partner," I said. "I don't know his name."

She left me alone after that, but before she left the room she did a funny thing. I'd left my panties on top of my jeans on the chair, and yellow and red streaks were showing. The nurse folded them in a way that all the mess wouldn't show. I didn't know who she was hiding them from.

The doctor gave me antibiotics and some cream for my vagina. He wanted to know how it happened.

"Things got carried away," I said. "That's all."

"Do you want to see the police?"

"No, I don't," I said. I didn't think he would have believed me if I told him I was the one who started it, that I was the one who chose Keel.

It was the truth. I had chosen him. I knew all the stories about him, and he was the one I went to. I knew he'd help me start any fire I wanted to start. At the time I thought I just wanted to hurt Del, but that was not all the truth. I wanted something for myself, too. What it was I couldn't name. I kept wanting to call it love, but it was more like obliteration.

I knew that even then.

IT HURT so bad to go to the bathroom that I hardly drank anything for the next few days. When I did pee, my urine burned the open places, and it was so sharp and hot that I could barely make myself stay on the toilet seat. I closed my eyes and pressed against the bathroom wall with my shoulder. As soon as I was done, I wiped everything away with a wet washcloth.

The whole thing scared me. I worried not just about the

pain, but also about everything being infected. I could not stop thinking of the black blood showing through my skin, the way that inner lip was swollen and bruised, and I could not stop thinking about the tear in my clitoris. I had a dream where I could see the cells in my skin. The cells were pink and egg-shaped. Sometimes they were small, and sometimes they were so big they took over the dream. When I woke up, I felt like I was going crazy with all the throbbing and aching in my body. I made myself more upset by pinching the mirror between my legs again — this time with the bedside lamp aimed right at me. When I saw the mess, I could not stop crying. So I cried for a while, and when I did stop, I didn't feel anything, just flat and blank.

I think I was crazy those few days. I broke apart. My head ached and my eyes burned all the time. I slept as much as I could and then I slept some more. I did not talk to anyone — not June, not my mom, certainly not Del. I don't know how long my craziness would have gone on, but then something happened.

I was lying in bed, trying to sleep again after sleeping almost all day. I could not turn off my thoughts about my body, though, or about Del, and I felt like my whole body was clenched in fear. I didn't know what else to do, so I started smoothing my own hair back from my face. I wasn't pretending it was Del's hand, but I wanted something to comfort me, and I tried to give it to myself.

And I guess I fell asleep like that, with my own hand at my face, because the next thing I knew, I felt someone brushing my hair back from my face, and I thought, *Good, Del's here and he understands.*

I lay and let myself feel the brushing, and then I knew it wasn't Del's hand on my face but the wing of a bird. It was so light. I closed my eyes to better feel the softness, and that's when I saw that it was an owl, and that he had his great wing over my face. All my worrying and crying was being brushed away, and I felt myself go calm beneath the feathers.

When I woke the next morning, I remembered everything. I knew I was probably just healing, but I could feel my pain was not nearly as bad, and it somehow seemed connected to the dream.

That was how I put myself to sleep for the next few nights: thinking of that great, soft wing. I puzzled over the dream — wondered what the owl meant, why he had come — but I did not puzzle over the feeling the dream gave me. I stopped worrying about my cells, and I let my body do its work. Something still ached inside of me when I thought of how I brought the whole thing on myself, and I still felt sick when I thought of Del and the new lie I'd have to tell him, but my body did not frighten me anymore. A piece of me had gone far away, but I was still there.

The needle in my brain stayed stuck on how I was the only one to blame for the mess, but one idea brought me some relief: if it was true that I was the one who chose Kevin Keel, it was also true that I was the only one who had to know. I knew I could take anything if I was alone, if it was just me who had to stand it.

18

AFTER five days, I could pee without crying, and I went back to Dreisbach's. Once I got there, though, I didn't know if I would make it through my shift or not. My stomach felt like it was a fist, and I dreaded turning and having to meet Kevin Keel's eyes.

Keel never came in. Instead, my old man showed up at my tables. He was tanked.

"What should I get you, beer or coffee?" I said.

He thought for a second, then waved his hand in the air. "Get me coffee. I had enough to drink."

When I came back to the table with two cups of coffee, my dad said, "Were you busy tonight?"

"Usual dinner crowd," I said, and sat down. I put my elbows on the table and held my coffee cup up between both my hands. My dad sat back in his chair and curled one hand around his cup. He spent so much time outside his skin was deep red. I thought his eyes looked like cool water in all that fire.

"Jesus Christ," he said. "This place is a goddamn hole."

I didn't think he came in just to insult my workplace, but I didn't know what he was doing there. Then I figured he just wanted to talk, because he said, "Yeah, shit, Vangie, I admire you coming back here night after night. It's not easy coming back to a place you hate. Jesus Christ, I know that."

"It's all right," I said. "It's a job."

"Are you doing all right, Vangie?"

"What do you mean?"

"I mean are you doing all right? Are you okay here?"

I panicked for a second, because I thought maybe he somehow knew something about Kevin Keel, but then I looked at his face and saw he didn't know anything. He was looped and he wanted to talk. That was all.

"I'm all right, Dad. I'm doing all right."

"Well, I never see you anymore."

"I'm okay."

"Truck running good?"

"The truck's fine."

I tried to meet his eyes so I could nod at him, but he just kept staring off. He got like that sometimes when he drank. Forlorn. I'd been seeing the look for years.

"You don't have to worry about me," I told him.

"Ah, the hell," he said. "I don't have anything better to do."

For a little while I let myself wonder what it would be like to have a father I could talk to, but I stopped myself. Still, there was something about my dad that I couldn't deny. A lot of times when I was little, he was the one who came to find me hiding under the bed after I got yelled at by my mom. If I was crying, he'd tell me to stop, since it made my blue eyes all red. I didn't know how he knew something was wrong with me that night, but he did. It meant something to me just to have him sitting there.

My dad and I sat together a little longer, not talking but just sitting. When I started to get customers again, my dad stood up, left me a five-dollar tip for his cup of coffee, and said, *You take care, honey.* Then he was gone.

AFTER THAT one night, I never went back to Dreisbach's. Whatever else I had to live through, I did not have to go through dreading Kevin Keel every day. Dreisbach's was a good job, though, and I hated to see it go begging, so I called June up and told her to apply.

"They'll need someone right away," I said. "They'd be too big, but I could give you my uniforms."

"What happened?"

"It's a long story," I said. "What do you think? Do you think you want the job?"

"It's got to be better than sewing shirt collars," June said. "But what are you going to do? Are you sure you want to quit?"

"I already quit," I said. "It's done. I'm going to hire on at the orchard."

I didn't say anything to her about Kevin, and I knew I wouldn't. I didn't want her to know how I'd drawn our lives together in a circle, hers and his and mine. I did tell her about how long Del was going to be in detox.

"You shouldn't be alone," she said. "Come out and stay over. Ray and Luke are in Potter County all next weekend."

"I don't know. I don't think so."

"Oh, come on. We'll get stoned. It'll be like the old days."

I told her I'd come out if I could, and then I hung up the phone. All I wanted to do was sleep, but when I did try to sleep, I could not stop hearing Keel's voice.

Good pussy doesn't just lie there.

Is it sore?

I'm almost done.

I could not get those words out of my mind, and I decided June was right — I should not be alone. Even though she was in some ways the last person I wanted to see, because she was connected to Kevin, she was still my best friend. So I made a promise to myself that no matter what I felt like when the day came, I would go and spend time with her. It seemed worth a few lies to keep her friendship and not have her know what I'd done.

That night I could not sleep, so I got up and went down to the kitchen. I didn't know what to do with myself. I played a couple of hands of solitaire, which seemed like the kind of thing a person should do if they were up late and couldn't sleep. But it didn't interest me, and after a while I stopped and just sat instead, playing with the salt and pepper shakers. I hadn't moved anything on the table since Del left. There was a grocery list he'd made for me for the next time I went shopping so I wouldn't forget the foods he liked. The list was all written in his bad spelling: *frys or tots, hamburger, lunch meet, cap crunch, corn, razors and shave cream, min. steak, ravioly.* The list was written on the back of an old note from him that said *dont do dishes I'll do when I get up.* At the time, I'd done what the note asked and left the dirty dishes for him — and then ended up washing them all a few days later when they were still sitting in the sink and starting to stink.

I both liked and didn't like seeing the list and the note. I liked seeing them because they were proof that Del had been here, that we had shared some sort of life, and I didn't like them because they made me wonder if he was coming back. In any case, seeing his handwriting made me feel alone.

Del's bone-handled knife also lay on the table. He carried it almost all the time, and I wondered why he hadn't taken it with him the night he disappeared. No matter how many times I saw that knife on the table or fished it out of Del's pocket before I washed his jeans, it always surprised me, and it always made me wonder. When Del carried it, did he think he would need to use it, or was it the kind of thing that just having it with you meant you surely would not need it? Did he believe he could use it against a person? Even if I'd had a knife when I was with Kevin Keel, I didn't know if I would have been able to use it.

The knife scared me, but I picked it up and released the

catch — careful because the last thing I wanted was a gash in my hand and more physical pain. I studied the blade and the handle a long time. I tried holding it different ways and felt the weight of it against my fingers. Then I pressed the blade back down with the palm of my hand against the blunt side until I could latch it again.

I knew so little about Del. I knew what his face and body looked like, I knew what his voice sounded like, I knew how he screwed and I knew how he slept, but I knew nothing about *him*. I knew a few things, yes — how much he hated his old man, that he liked to draw and hated to hunt — but that was all. If I ever asked him what he was like when he was little, he'd say, "I don't know. A regular kid. I don't remember." Whenever he did tell me some kind of story, it was about a time he stole something or got in trouble. I knew nothing of how he got to be the person he was with me.

But I didn't know how I got to be the person I was, either.

19

Aᴛ Parmelee Orchard, I didn't need to fill out an application or have an interview — the place hired anyone who showed up in the orchard yard. Anyone crazy enough to pick over a ton of pears a day for minimum wage could have a job.

When my dad found out what I was doing, he said, "Jesus Christ, Vangie, that kind of work'll break your back if you do it all your life."

"I'm not going to do it all my life."

"Be glad you have your diploma, then, and don't have to. Women who work like that — that's why they look the way they do. They're wore out."

When he said it, I thought he was trying to discourage me, but by the end of the first day of work, I knew he had just been telling me the truth. I had to pick about one hundred bags of pears a day — twenty-five hundred pounds — just to make minimum wage, and I did not get anything beyond minimum wage unless I broke the hundred-bag mark. That was the amount of fruit the orchard set as its daily standard for ground crew. Even though the standard was a little less for ladder crew — eighty bags — it was lucky for me they put most of the women on ground crew. At least we did not have to lug old, rotting wood ladders through the orchard rows.

When you picked a pear, you did not tug it or yank it. You lifted it. The pear was attached to the tree by a ball-and-socket joint, "the same kind of joint you have in your hip," the orchard boss told us. To pick the pear, you lifted until that joint broke. The stem/leg came away with the pear, and the hip stayed on the tree. The joint was the easiest thing to break if you knew how, and not so easy if you didn't. Of course I became expert at it. Every pear I picked, I slipped into the picking sack I wore strapped around my neck and waist. When I had a full sack, I emptied the pears into one of the packing crates in the orchard rows, and the foreman punched my count card.

That picking sack was a hell of a thing. It was really what made the job hard. The sack was said to hold twenty-five pounds of pears, and I knew from the feel of it that it held at least that amount. But if I had a few extra pears in there — if the foreman sent me back to the trees because he thought my bag needed a few more pears to level off — I knew I could easily be carrying twenty-six or twenty-seven pounds. That was all to the orchard's advantage, because they were only paying me for twenty-five. But I guessed if I wanted a job with an exact science, I probably shouldn't have been working at Parmelee Orchard.

When my sack was full of pears, it was easy to want to arch my back and give in to the weight, especially if I'd been working a few hours. Joe Spancake, the foreman, was always after us to walk straight up, and he harangued us when we dumped off our pears.

"Don't be walking like pregnant women, now. Pull your hips in under you and your backs won't hurt so much."

Most of the time I was good about not arching, but when I was tired or wasn't thinking, I gave in to the bag. If Joe caught me, he'd cinch the picking bag tighter to my waist so the weight would be as close to my body as possible, and so the tightness would remind me.

"That ought to do you for a while," he'd say.

After two days, I could clear out the bottom of a tree in a few minutes, so Joe turned me and a couple other women out into the rows first, and we set the pace for the whole crew. I got so I could pick with both hands going, my eyes scanning the branches for the next pear, bringing the green fruit into my sack by feel. It was hard to pick that fast and talk, so I really did not talk to any of the other women on the crew until breaks. By the end of the third day I broke the hundred bags a day mark with 106 bags of pears, and by the start of my second week at work, I was picking over 120 bags a day — over three thousand pounds of pears.

I started picking at seven in the morning and worked on through to four-thirty, with a half hour for lunch and two fifteen-minute breaks. In the morning, the dew was so heavy on the grass that my feet got soaked and the skin of my toes turned white and peeled from the dampness. My dad told me to get waterproof work boots, and that helped that end of things, but there was nothing I could do about the way the straps of my picking sack dug into my neck. Oh, I could wrap a towel around the straps to try to pad them, but in a little while the towel was wet and would rub at my neck anyway.

But I would not quit. Something in me liked to work that hard. My fingers got nicked and rough from the picking, I got calluses on my neck from where the straps of the picking sack rubbed, and I could feel how strained my neck and back were sometimes, but that was all part of it. I could do the work, no matter how hard, and something about that made me glad.

Because the monotony of the day would have grown if I only looked forward to its end, I learned to enjoy the bits that could be enjoyed: the cool breeze that came through the orchard rows in the first part of the morning; the good taste of the first green pear I ate during the day; the time in the morning when the coolness stopped and sun warmed my back between the straps of my picking bag; the curious way my arms and hands felt at the end of the day, after picking for eight hours — so light I might have flown away. On our water breaks, Joe Spancake sometimes brought his dogs into the rows, and if I had a chance to sit for fifteen minutes — drinking warm water from a shared cup, leaning back against my sack and hugging on a dog — I felt happy. I did not think about anything except how good it was to sit on the warm ground in the shade of a pear tree, or how much I loved whatever crazy dog was by me — the Lab dark as a Hershey bar, or the golden one who liked to put his big front paws on my sleeves. Kevin Keel did not enter my mind, and Del's overdose did not enter my mind, and my own lies did not enter my mind. I didn't think of anything that hurt.

The orchard wasn't anything like Noecker's. Even though I picked pears all day long and carried over a ton of them around on my belly each day like I was pregnant with the lumpiest, greenest, hardest baby, I never stopped liking pears. They were the best thing to cool thirst on a hot afternoon. In some ways, eating a green pear was even better than drinking water, because the taste of a green pear was easy going down in a way that the metal taste of the orchard water was not. Sometimes we found yellow pears under the trees, splitting open in brown stripes, and some women on the crew coveted them. Not me. I only wanted green.

THOUGH DEL was not permitted telephone calls, he was allowed to write, and not long into his treatment, I started getting letters. The first ones were short and were about what his days were like, but it was not long before he started writing about sex. After he started that, I didn't hear too much about group anymore, or about how he had to wash the floors as part of his communal contribution. Instead he wrote:

God I miss having sex with you and 69 too. When you have my cock in your mouth and you hum, I don't know why that does it for me but it does every time. My cocks hard just remembering. As days go on all I can think about is when I will see you again. What is the first thing you want me to do Vangie? Will you want me to lick your pussy untill you come? Sometimes I think what its like when I have my toungue inside you and I almost come from thinking of it.

Well Vangie are you wet now? I've re-read your last letter a few times and even though I know what your gonna say I get a hard cock for you every time. I miss your smell and taste of your pussy, its like I need it or I can't sleep right. Miss you and love you. Your lover, Del.

I read his letters over, too, and sometimes they turned me on, and sometimes I thought, God, all we talk about is fucking. The letters made me feel both close to Del and farther away from him than ever. I tried to explain to him what I meant, and he said this:

Its hard to talk about things because I'm here but, I understand what your saying. No it is not just fucking between us, though I miss that. To me you are ideal. No one knows me better than you and I know you are the only girl I ever really loved. I said that word before to others but, it was wrong. I know that now. You can put things better than me but I hope you understand me now. If not we will have to talk about things when I get back.

Other than that I miss your kisses and your warm wet pussy and you sucking my cock! Ha ha, no I miss everything about you. I promise that when I get done here you'll trust me and things will be different. I hope you fuck the hell out of your self and come for me. Maybe you'll come all over the next letter you write me. I love you, Del.

And after I healed, I did masturbate, over and over. I wanted to prove to myself that my body was the same as before. Those orgasms were just for me, though. I never did come on a piece of paper to send to Del.

2 0

L u k e and Ray kept changing the weekend they were going to Potter County, so when I finally went out to stay with June, it was a month after the night I fucked her brother. I was long done with my antibiotics, and the little tears in my skin had healed. The little split at the base of my clitoris had healed that way — a tiny forked place.

I did not have to tell June anything about the OD, because by then she already knew the story, like everyone in Mahanaqua: Del had been found in someone's yard after he walked away from a party.

"Do you hear from him a lot?" June asked. "Is he doing all right?"

"He's all right. They're making him talk about his feelings."

"What was going on with him?"

"I don't know. I'd be the last one to know."

"What do you mean?"

"I don't know what I mean," I said. "Tell me about you."

"Vangie."

"I don't want to talk about it," I said. "I came out to get stoned with you. You talk."

"What do you want to know?"

"Everything," I said.

"All right. I stopped it all for a while. How's that?"

"What did you stop?"

"All of it. He was doing crazy stuff. Luke. So I stopped everything. Went home for a couple days."

She said the three of them had been at a party and Luke kept trying to kiss her in the upstairs hallway, even though Ray was just downstairs. When she'd pulled away from him, Luke just laughed at her. Later, when she went outside for air, Luke followed her and tried to pull her to him again.

"I said to him, 'Don't you feel anything? Ray's just inside. He's not stupid.' And he said, 'He's not stupid, but he doesn't know a thing about you.'"

"What did you do?"

"I told him I wasn't the one who started it. And he said, 'You didn't turn it down, either.' I didn't sleep with him for two weeks after he said that."

"But you're sleeping with the two of them now."

"I know."

She stopped talking then, and we just sat there at the table, drinking. The whole house was quiet.

"Why don't you leave Ray?" I said. "You haven't ever really loved him, have you?"

"I love him. I don't love him the way I love Luke, but I care for him."

"They're brothers."

"They were both strangers to me."

"June," I said. I waited a bit and then I said, "You can't keep playing the game."

"It's not a game."

"Then what is it?"

She didn't answer, but for the first time I understood that she had no intention of leaving Ray. Luke might be her true love, but she had no intention of choosing. Ray was part of it, part of the whole weave of things, and she wanted to go on living it.

"You'll have to do something sooner or later," I said.

"It isn't that easy, Vangie."

"It's easier than you're making it."

But all she would say to that was, "Maybe."

She started talking about Dreisbach's then. She didn't tell me any more about Luke or Ray. I didn't talk about Del, and it goes without saying that I didn't talk about how I fucked her brother.

Probably because it was the easiest thing to do, we decided to get high. As we were smoking up, I told her all the tips I knew about working at Dreisbach's: about hemming her skirts up and about my regulars and how to squeeze a dollar out of people. Because it was easier to talk about jobs and work than anything else, that is what we talked about then, and I did not feel bad about it. She updated me on the latest gossip at the restaurant, and I told her about the joy of picking pears. At least we could laugh and joke. That was the same as it ever was between us.

When we had enough to smoke, June said, "Come on. Let's go to bed."

She took me upstairs to Luke's room, but I couldn't quite believe she wanted us to sleep there.

"I can sack out on the sofa," I said.

"Don't be crazy, Vangie. This is the best bed in the house."

And it was some bed. It was king-size, and the frame was all oak. It was massive. The headboard had built-in cupboards, one on each side, and each cupboard closed with its own lead-glass door. In between the two cupboards was a huge mirror.

"Jesus Christ," I said. "It's like a football field."

"He had to bring it in the house in pieces," June said.

Of course I snooped in the cupboard on my side of the bed as soon as we lay down, because I wanted to see the kind of stuff Luke kept there. I found some magazines, a box of tissues, a clock, and a gun.

I knew the thing was loaded. There would be no point to keep a gun that ready at the bedside if it wasn't loaded.

"What is that?" I said.

"A .38 Special."

"I don't know if I can sleep with that there."

The pistol was black and heavy-looking, and it made me feel sick just to see it.

"I mean it," I told June. "I can't sleep with it there."

"Here," she said, and took one of the magazines. She opened it and laid it over the gun. "Now you can't see it."

"I don't know if that's going to do it," I said.

"I'll put it on my side, then."

The pistol looked crazy in June's hand, and I was glad she was the one who picked it up. I didn't even want to touch it.

"Don't think about it," June said, and closed the cupboard door.

I was almost sorry then that I was staying over. I felt stoned and unsure, my nerves were still jangling from everything that had happened with Kevin Keel, and the gun just upset me. I began to worry that June or I would wake in the night and, in some crazy dream, reach out and make the gun go off. I didn't think we would shoot each other — I just thought we would somehow knock the pistol out of the cupboard and that it would somehow fire and hurt one of us. Even though it was on June's side of the bed, I worried that I might do something crazy and clumsy because I was so afraid. That is what I lay thinking of in that big bed.

"Should I show you something of mine?"

"Sure," I said. I thought, great, she's got a matching pearl-handled pistol or something on her side. But what June pulled out was a little tan thing that looked like a small hair dryer. I didn't know what it was at first, but then I remembered seeing one in a magazine, and it all dawned on me about what it was.

"I keep it here," she said. "I only use it with Luke. Ray couldn't handle it."

She flicked the switch on the top and the thing turned on. It whirred like a bug. I put my hand out to touch the piece that moved.

"It looks like a nose," I said.

"It sort of is like a nose," she said. "You can use it if you want."

She turned off the bedside light then, but I cannot remember how it happened next, the order of things: if she moved her hand down between my legs and then I parted them, or if I parted my legs first.

"Is that the place?"

I moved my hips a little, and then it was the right place. She only touched me a few seconds and she said, "It's better if you take off your underwear."

And there in the prickling darkness I did that. And that time I know I was the one who moved first, who spread my legs apart so she could get to me.

The little nose piece was so insistent, the buzz so hard, that my skin seemed to draw back. But only for a little while. Pretty soon the buzz was not so hard, and I could feel the tension easing, and all the tightness went into a contraction I had up inside me, and that happened over and over. I came fast and hard in a few minutes.

I did not make a sound, but June knew. She was on the other end of that plastic thing — of course she knew.

"You and Del should get one," she said. "Do you want to use it anymore?"

"No, thanks."

"All right. Do you mind if I do?"

"I don't mind," I said. "Go ahead."

She turned a little to face the wall, for privacy, the way we did when we had hickeys to hide.

"Do you want me to go?" I said.

"No. No, you don't have to go."

It didn't take June that long to come. She did not make any sound. The only reason I knew she did was that her breathing got harder. A few seconds later she turned off the vibrator and put it back in the cupboard, then turned so she could lie on her belly.

"Are you still awake?"

"I'm awake."

"Young and dumb and full of come," she said. "I'm sorry, Vangie. I just had to do that. You came and then I wanted to."

"You don't have to apologize. It's me."

The next thing I said, I could not account for. I felt worried about her being in that house with Luke and Ray, I wished everything could be different for the two of us, and I was glad to be lying there with her, away from the bed I shared with Del and my own life. But I still could not account for what I said, and I could not tell where it came from.

I said to June, "I wish I could be your boyfriend."

I lay and waited in the dark to hear what she would say, and when she did talk, her voice was filled with kindness.

"I know what you mean."

"No, I really wish I could."

"Oh, Vangie," she said, and her voice was still so filled with kindness that I felt she knew what I meant.

"But you can't be."

"I know," I said, and in the sticking darkness I suddenly wasn't so sure that she knew all the things I wanted for her and for me, or that she knew what I meant at all.

"I still wish it," I said.

She did not answer, but moved back against me so her back was resting lightly against my arm and hip. That made me feel better, even though she didn't talk, and even though I knew she wanted me not to talk.

That night, I surprised myself by sleeping. I slept hard at first, then my dreams woke me. I kept seeing the .38 Special and June reaching up into the cupboard. She brought something down between my legs, and I kept thinking it was the gun. I'd worry that it would fire, but then it would turn out not to be the gun at all. Sometimes it was that hard, plastic knob touching me, and sometimes it was her hand. It all got mixed up in my mind.

21

T H A T week I could not stop thinking about what happened with June. The thoughts took over the ones about Kevin Keel and those about Del, and I didn't fight them. I let my mind go back again and again to the night I spent with her. I could not stop thinking of the little plastic nose moving over me, or how deep my contractions had been when I came. It felt like they started at the very core of me and kept on reaching out and out and out. I could not have stopped thinking of that if I tried.

With its beige nose, the vibrator wasn't at all like a dildo. It was something altogether different, and I wondered how June had learned about it. I wondered if Luke bought it for her, or if she saw it in a magazine the way I did. But if she just saw it in a magazine, how did she know it would be right for her body, right for coming? And why had she wanted to touch me with it? Because that's how I thought of it, as June touching me, even though there was that plastic between us. Maybe it was like the old days when we wrote notes and recounted each detail of being with Del and Ray: maybe she had just wanted to show me her new trick. Except I remembered how her voice sounded when she said, *Is that the place?* All murmury and soft. It was like my voice when I was being sweet with Del. Yet June's voice sounded the same way after I told her I wished I could be her boyfriend and she said, *But you can't be* — so I didn't know what to think of the softness. Maybe it didn't mean anything. Maybe it just meant that we were talking quietly in the darkness.

It took me a couple of days to realize I was not embarrassed by June touching me. If I'd felt any kind of embarrassment, I wouldn't have been able to come. I knew that in my body. What embarrassed me was what I said: *I wish I could be your boyfriend.* Yet as I thought of my words, I wondered about them. At the time I meant that I felt closer to June than anyone in the world, and that I wanted us to look out for each other and go on caring for each other always. But when I realized I was not embarrassed about June touching me or about her making me come, I wondered if part of me wasn't in love with June, and if that wasn't what I'd been saying that night. Maybe what embarrassed me wasn't what I said at all, but what she told me in return: *You can't be.*

After I understood that, I did not want to talk to her.

I tried not to make it seem obvious, but June knew something was wrong. We were on the phone when she asked me what was going on.

"I feel funny," I said. "A little uncomfortable."

"What, because of last weekend? It doesn't matter."

I didn't know if she was saying that it didn't matter that the two of us used her vibrator and that she made me come, or if it didn't matter that I said I wanted to be her boyfriend. Both things mattered to me, but I couldn't say that, so I told her, "It's hard for me to see you out there with the two of them." It wasn't entirely a lie.

"I know you think it's wrong."

"That's not even it," I said. "I don't understand how you go on. Don't you worry?"

"No," she said. "You don't know how safe I feel."

She went on to tell me about a photograph of Luke and Ray, one that she'd seen at their mom and dad's house and that she'd thought about for months. Luke and Ray were standing with their mother and father, out in front of the house where they grew up. June said that one day when she was looking at that picture, she thought she understood what she was doing.

"No one can ever get closer to them than me," she said. "Not even their parents. I'm there between them."

"June, it's a picture."

"If you saw it, if you knew how I felt when I saw it, you'd understand. I know you would."

"Maybe," I said.

"You would. I know. You're like a sister to me."

"And you to me," I said, but as soon as I said it, I felt let down. It seemed we were marking an end.

After that conversation, we turned away from each other. No, that's still not the truth. I turned away from June, and she had no choice but to turn away from me. At the time it seemed the right thing to do, because I didn't want to embarrass her further, and because I didn't want her to say, ever, that she didn't want to hear from me. But let me put down here that it was me who had the small heart and it was me who turned away.

There. Now it is all written down.

In the days that followed that conversation, I thought of what June said about the photograph of Ray and Luke. How she said she felt safe when she saw it. Her words were a maze that I was not sure I found the heart of, but I thought she meant this:

The picture was a whole. Whether the parents smiled or not, whether they put a hand on the shoulder of each boy, whether one brother threw an arm around the other or they simply stood shoulder to shoulder — none of it mattered. Happy or sad, touching or not touching, the picture was a record of who was bound to whom. That was why people wasted roll after roll of film on stiff poses and artificial smiles: they wanted a picture, if not of their love, at least of their blood.

Without being in that picture, June came to rest at the center of it, between the two brothers. She was stitched into them and between them. Nothing could ever take her out, and that was her power. That was why she didn't stop, and that was why she could feel safe, even in the middle of all the lies and the danger. She believed she could go on floating between two brothers. In dark water, cradled.

2 2

——

D EL came home that week
after being gone six — one week bingeing, one week in
detox, and four weeks in treatment. Even though it was only
about eight at night, we went to bed almost as soon as he
walked in the door.

When we lay down on the bed, I tried to act like nothing
was different, like things were the way they always were. We
kissed slow and deep, and I kept running my hand over Del's
back and the railing of his spine. It soothed me to be with
his bare skin and to be touching again, but then I'd get aware
of myself and everything that had happened, and I'd feel
wooden.

When Del pulled away from me and started to move down on the bed so he could lie with his face between my legs, I put my arms tight around him. I made him lie back down.

"How about a birthday blow job?" I said, because he'd had his twentieth birthday when he was in treatment. But that wasn't why I was offering it — I wasn't ready for him to touch my vagina.

"All right," he said, and he pressed his cock up into my breasts and then against my face. He was so anxious to have me touch him that he could not lie still. Usually he let me set the pace and the depth, but not that time. He kept lifting his hips and pushing into the roof of my mouth and the back of my throat. He came in no time, and it was so far back in my throat I couldn't even taste it.

After, we lay together, and he touched my face and wrapped his hands in my hair.

"You all right?"

"I'm okay," I said.

"You sure?"

"It just made my nose run."

We lay together not talking, then Del said, "Bring your puss up here."

"We can wait."

"What, do you have your period?"

I didn't say anything, and he moved his hand down to the soft part of my belly, waiting.

"I don't care if there's blood," he said, reaching down to touch the hair. "I ate you before like that."

"I'm not bleeding. It's not that."

"Then let me. I've been waiting six weeks for some pussy."

"Could you just slow down?" I said. "Just give me a chance?"

"Give you a chance? What do you mean?"

I couldn't tell him the truth about Kevin Keel or my scar, and I also couldn't tell him how he seemed like a stranger to me just then. Even though he just came in my throat, I felt that I hardly knew him.

"I just have to get used to you again," I said. As soon as I said the words, I knew I'd hurt him, and I knew he'd have to hurt me back.

"What the fuck, Vangie? I waited six weeks for you and that's all you can say?"

"I waited six weeks for you, too."

"You don't act like it. What's wrong with you anyway? You used to like to get your pussy fucked."

"I'm glad you're home," I said, trying to make my voice steady. "I just need to get used to being with you again."

"What's there to get used to?"

"Everything," I said. "All of it." I did not say, *You.*

We lay there not touching, not talking, and after a while, I sat up. I could tell from Del's silence that he thought I was moving away from him, getting out of bed. But that's not what I did. I got on my hands and knees, facing away from him, so he could see my ass and between my legs. I knew he was watching me, and I knew it was all I needed to do. I wanted to end the fight, and I knew I could do it more easily with my body than I could with my voice.

"What's that for?"

"I want you."

"Do you?" he said. "You want some of my cock?"

I wanted him to get up inside me and erase anything left from Kevin Keel. I didn't want to see his face while he did it, and I didn't want him to see mine. And I wanted to stop thinking.

"Tell me, Vangie. Tell me you want some of my cock."

I didn't say anything at first, just went on kneeling and letting him look at me. Then I started rocking back and forth, arching my back and rubbing my breasts over the sheet.

"I want you to fuck me," I told him.

As soon as I said it, he moved into me.

Even as I was grunting under his weight, or reaching out to slip my hand between his hips and my cunt so I could feel the root of his cock, I'd get a flash in my mind of Kevin Keel. But I pushed the thought from my mind, and I pushed it from my mind, and in the end it stayed away.

Del had an orgasm in a couple minutes. It wasn't like the nights when he was drunk and could fuck for an hour without coming. This was probably one of the few times he fucked me sober.

"You scared me there for a minute," Del said after a bit. "I thought you didn't like to screw anymore."

When I didn't answer, Del said, "No, that's a lie. I didn't think that."

"What did you think?"

"I thought you didn't like me anymore."

I didn't say anything, but I squeezed him with the muscles inside me and bumped back against him. He still seemed like a stranger to me, but there was no way for me to explain that to him. Anyway, maybe I was the stranger. While we were apart, things had happened to me, too.

We lay together for a while and Del got soft inside me. He slipped out, slip, just like that, and when he moved off me, he said, "I'm going to wake you up in the middle of the night and make you come. You need it, too."

I felt a little of his come seeping out of me, and I rolled onto my side to grab a handful of tissues from the box on the floor.

"I took care of myself while you were gone," I said.

"Did you?"

"A little."

"You lie, Vangie. You probably masturbated every night."

I thought about how close he was to the truth, and how far, but there was no point in thinking like that. "I didn't do it every night," I said. "But I did do it."

"I'm glad. I'm glad you took care of yourself."

When he said that, he sounded like Del, and I felt bad. I thought of all the times he'd made me come and how happy he always was when it happened. No one loved me as much as he did, and I'd hardly thought of him the past week. All I'd been thinking of was June.

"Don't think I forgot my promise to you, either, Vangie," Del said to me then.

"What promise?"

"That you'll trust me this time."

We could have said *I love you,* and *I love you, too,* but we didn't. We just settled into sleep — Del on his back, me on my belly — the house dark around us, all my secrets safe.

23

ALL Del ever told me about the overdose was how the last thing he remembered was falling down and feeling the rain in his face. He never told me where he got the quaaludes, who he'd done them with, or how it all felt. Still, I knew the OD scared Del. He was scared so bad he got religion.

I guess I shouldn't have found it so hard to believe. His family was born again, but it was the first time Del was ever interested. He started talking a lot about a higher power, and he began going to church with his family. Even though I didn't believe in any of it, I thought it would be helpful for Del and me to want the same things, so I went with him to church. I told myself that if anything positive happened, I would not rule it out.

I did that a whole month: sat with my heart as open as I could get it to feel, waiting for some feeling of God to come. I didn't know what I expected to happen — a flutter, a warmth, a happiness. Something. But of course I felt nothing.

"I don't know," I said to Del one Sunday when we were driving to the church for another hour of talk about pain and suffering. "It makes me feel worse to go on sitting there, waiting for something that never happens."

"You just need to keep trying. God knows what's in your heart," Del said. His voice sounded so calm and weird that I turned to look at him, but he just kept driving.

He used that same strange voice to testify in church the next Sunday. At a certain point in the service, anyone could stand up and speak about how God was touching their lives, and that was called testifying. Del stood up, thanked everyone for helping him pass through hard times, and spoke a little about how lost he'd been when he was drinking and drugging. He said that all the people who surrounded him had been lost, too, and that he was glad he found a way to free himself from them and find God.

I couldn't believe it. To me it seemed foolish to let people know that much about you, and dangerous to declare you were on a path so different from the one you'd walked for so long. But what really bothered me was that according to Del's definition I was "lost" because I still hadn't found that born-again God.

On the way home I was silent, but Del did not seem to notice. He took my hand and said, "Pretty soon you can start testifying, too. You've been through as much as me."

"I don't think so," I said.

"It's hard at first. Then it feels okay."

"I don't think it's my style."

"People will listen to you, Vangie. They're with you when you're talking."

He didn't need to tell me that — I'd heard all the amens and seen all the nodding heads.

I said, "I don't want anyone listening to me. I don't have anything to say."

"You will. You'll find all kinds of things to say."

It was like there was this one plan, and he was just waiting for it to be revealed to me, and for me to go along with it. Even though Del was taking it seriously, I knew I couldn't. Wearing my ironed skirts and pretending like I somehow regretted all the drugs and drinking and the fucking that went with them — it was just play for me. No church service could help me with the things I needed help with, and after working all week and moving seven tons of pears, I didn't think I had to bow my head down to anyone.

Even though I could barely stand the low feelings Sundays gave me, I decided to keep my mouth shut for a while for Del's sake. He seemed to be getting something out of it, and I didn't want to do anything to derail him. I told myself that except for Sundays, none of the born-again stuff really affected our lives. Del and I still fucked all the time — until our pelvis bones hurt, until I was raw and Del's balls ached from banging against me. I didn't think any of it was what the Christians had in mind for us, but Del didn't seem to see the conflict.

I was suspicious of the whole religion thing, but I was also suspicious of Del. I wondered how a person could make such a drastic change so quickly. Where did all the craziness in him go to? Did it just disappear? Where was the part of him that came home in the middle of the day and needed to huff PAM in the kitchen? Where was the part of him that bit and squeezed my breasts until he bruised the skin black?

I didn't miss that crazy person, but I wondered where he went all the same.

IN TIME, the vast number of secrets I was keeping began to eat away at me. I lied whenever I didn't tell Del that June was fucking Ray's brother. I lied every time I didn't tell Del about his own brother and me. And of course I lied every time I got into bed with Del and didn't tell him about Kevin Keel.

The lie about Kevin Keel was so dark that it began to work on me in funny ways. Sometimes in the middle of the night I would have to get up from bed and go to the bathroom and pinch a mirror between my legs. I worried that in having sex with Del, I would somehow reopen or infect my scar. I couldn't stop thinking about it, and I got to the point where I was checking myself two and three times a day. When I started having orgasms again, I got even worse, because I worried that when my clitoris swelled up a little from being excited, the scar might get bigger, too. I felt a little crazy, and I felt like it was getting harder and harder to hide it all from Del.

One night after I came wetly on Del's mouth — the first time I came that way since he got home — I was terrified. I climbed off him right away and lay with my head down by his feet. He kept his fingers on me, though, playing with me, and when I heard him go to speak, I was sure he would ask me about that little forked place. But instead he said, "Can I get you pregnant?"

After I understood he wasn't asking me about the scar, I said, "What are you talking about? You know I'm on the pill."

"No, I mean can I get you pregnant? Can I knock you up?"

His voice was all full of hope, and for a minute I thought he was drunk again, that's how crazy it all sounded.

"I want to knock you up. I've been thinking of marrying you, Vangie, and I want to knock you up."

"You're crazy."

"No, I'm not. Go off the pill. I want to put a kid inside you."

"Are you saying this just to get me wet?" I asked, because the whole time he was talking, he was playing with me.

"I'm serious, Vangie. I want to come home from work every day and see you like that."

"You are out of your motherfucking mind," I said. "I am not interested in a baby."

"You will be. And you will go off the pill." He said it just like that, the same way he told me I would testify. Like it was a simple matter of time until his will overtook mine.

Because Del couldn't get inside me fast enough after he said that, I figured it was all a new kind of sex talk. Since he wasn't drinking or smoking weed anymore and couldn't fuck for hours, he had to take off in a new direction in his fantasies. The new fantasy somehow involved me being pregnant, and I thought it had to do with being born again and the sober life he was trying to lead. He'd stopped drinking and was going to church, and maybe he thought that having a baby and settling down was the next step.

A baby was the last thing I wanted. I figured I'd be a disaster at raising it, just the way my folks were, and I didn't care if I had to take Lo/Ovral the rest of my life to avoid it. There were times I even thought of getting sterilized, because the idea of having a baby scared me so bad. But the scariest thing about listening to Del talk about getting me pregnant was something I could hardly admit to myself, and I got sick when I realized that I liked the way his voice sounded when he said, *I've been thinking of marrying you, Vangie, and I want to knock you up.*

Even though I was terrified by the idea of having a baby, I could feel a thirsty place in me that had drunk in those words and the kind, hopeful sound of Del's voice as he said them. It was just a little place in me, but I could feel it all the same.

2 4

JUST as d'Anjou season was finishing, Joe Spancake asked me if I wanted to run a stand at Daubert's Farmers Market, over in Nila Gap. It was a start-up sort of a deal, Joe said, until they saw if it would fly. I'd work three ten-hour shifts by myself and be responsible for loading up the truck every morning and bringing back unsold produce at the end of the day. At first I didn't know what to think, then I got glad thinking about the change. So I said yes.

"It's not a sure thing," Joe said. "I have to clear it with the owner. I'm just feeling you out."

But he kept telling me how I'd be perfect for the job at Daubert's because I was "good with the public," which I figured was a reference to my waitressing days, and when the owner agreed to give me the job, I think Joe was happier than I was.

"You're just the right person, Vangie."

I went, "Yeah, think of it. First waiting tables and now this. Who knows how far I could go?"

I thought Joe would lay into me for being a smartass, but he just looked at me for a moment.

"Is there something else you'd rather be doing?" he said.

From the way he said it, I knew the question was nothing more and nothing less than what it seemed.

"There isn't anything else I'd rather be doing," I said, and meant it.

I was to be at the stand from eight to six every day the market was open — Tuesdays, Thursdays, and Saturdays — which meant leaving the orchard with my truck loaded no later than seven in the morning. Since I would be running the stand by myself, when I had to go to the toilet during the day, I'd put up a sign that said "Back in 5 minutes," take my money pouch, and leave the stand. Customers who wanted to buy fruit would either wait, circle back on their second pass through the market, or buy from some other stand.

"Don't you worry about someone taking something?" I asked Joe when he told me the setup.

"No one walks off with a bushel or a peck of fruit," he said. "Don't worry."

I remembered the farmers market from times my mom and dad dragged me along with them, and the first day I walked in, I saw the place had not changed at all. The whole of it was a series of old barns with concrete floors, with doors here and there opening to the outside. What a joint it was! The whole place had a funny, rank smell, which was in part from the fruits and vegetables, in part from the blood at the butcher counter, and in part from the hot people working the stands or shopping in the aisles.

Still, I liked the place. I liked to be in the bustle of things. I liked to watch the country people who came in for their weekly shopping trips, and I liked watching the people who ran the stands. There were produce stands, pie and baked goods stands, a funnel cake stand, a stand selling the homeliest kind of farm-wife blouses and dresses, and a jewelry stand selling bracelets, necklaces, and bolo ties made of a metal that lasted a wearing or two before turning sour and gray.

My favorite stands were the ones the Mennonites ran, but that was because I liked to watch the Mennonite boys work. Unlike the girls, who were mainly chunky and homely, the Mennonite boys were almost all good-lookers. I didn't like the young married men — I thought the fringe of beard they wore made them look silly — but the teenage boys and the unmarried ones my age caught my eye. They had slim hips and thick shoulders from the work they did, and their soft blue or green shirts looked pretty against their tanned skins. Something about seeing all those strong waists rising up out of pants that weren't cinched around by a belt — well, it did it for me.

So even though it had made me laugh to hear Joe Span-cake talk about how I was good with the public, or to have him say that I had the best attendance of any picker he ever knew, I was glad he got me the job. I liked talking with people who stopped by the stand, I liked making the bushel and peck baskets look nice, and I liked the change apron I wore. I knew I would not have been picked to run the stand if I was a fuck-up, so the whole experience was like getting an award at school, which I never got, or like pulling in some half-decent tips at Dreisbach's. Plus, the job was about a hundred times easier than picking pears, and I knew I was lucky to be out of the orchard rows.

Still, I missed seeing the trees of the orchard, and crazily, I even missed wearing the picking sack around my neck and waist. When I had the sack on, I felt strong, and when I took it off at the end of the day, I felt like I put my burden aside. It was a powerful combination of feelings, and I knew I couldn't explain to anyone what it meant to me. But those first steps without the sack after wearing it all day — well, I could have sworn I was airborne.

NOT LONG after I started running the stand at the farmers market, Del took to giving me a baby talk every night as I stood in front of the bathroom sink and punched a Lo/Ovral pill from its plastic cap into my hand.

"No one's ever ready for kids," he was saying this particular night. "And you know I love you. I want to knock you up."

"What you should do is knock it off. I do not want a baby."

"When are you going to believe I'm serious?"

"Oh, I know you're serious," I said. "But I'm serious, too. I'm not ready for a baby."

"When do you think you will be ready?"

"I don't know. But a long time from now."

I waited awhile there at the sink, putting cream on my face, and then I went, "Maybe some people shouldn't ever be ready. Take my old man. He probably never should have had kids. When my mom got pregnant with me, you know what he did? He didn't take a shower for three weeks. He was mad at her for getting pregnant. As if she did it herself."

"Well, your dad's crazy."

"What about your dad? You said yourself he never wanted any of you."

"You can't judge us by them," Del said. "Besides, I'll do a damn sight better than my dad did. He never stopped drinking. I'm already a step ahead."

Then, because I could not stand the thought of getting preached at some more, and because I didn't even know how to talk to Del these days, I said, "I had a funny dream last night."

I told Del my dream of the owl, the dream I had after I fucked Kevin Keel, which I hadn't told anyone, but which I still hadn't forgotten. I was lying by saying I had the dream the night before, but everything else I said about the dream was true: how I'd heard the beating of wings and saw the striped markings, how the bird flew close to me and brushed my hair back with one wing.

At the end I said, "When the owl brushed its wing over

my face, the whole thing felt real. I mean, I could really feel feathers against my face. It made me happy. Comforted, you know? And that was the dream. It was something."

Del looked at me a long time after I finished, and I couldn't read his face. He looked half surprised and half mad, but when he started to talk, I realized it wasn't anger at all that I was seeing.

"The Holy Spirit comes in different forms, Vangie. It's the sign you've been waiting for."

He said it in that calm Christ-voice that made me crazy.

"How do you know it's the Holy Spirit?" I said.

"It had wings, it came down upon your head. What else could it be?"

"A bird. Maybe the dream was just about a bird," I said. I wanted to go on and tell him the truth about when I had the dream and how it had nothing at all to do with church or being born again, but if I confessed to one lie, it might make my other lies harder to uphold. So I said nothing, not about when I really had my dream, not about my scar, and not about Kevin Keel.

"Why are you rejecting Him, Vangie? Isn't this the sign you've been waiting for?"

"The only sign I'm waiting for is when you're going to get tired of the whole thing."

"What whole thing?"

"This whole God thing. The going to church, the testifying, all that Bible study stuff."

"I can't believe you," Del said, shaking his head.

"Well believe me. My dream was about a bird."

"Anyone else would be happy to get a sign from the Holy Spirit."

"I'm happy I dreamed about a bird. How's that?"

"Fucking-A, Vangie. Why can't you just accept it?"

He hadn't gotten mad about all the Sundays I bitched about having to get up early, and he hadn't gotten mad about me refusing to testify, but me dreaming about an owl and calling it a bird instead of the Holy Spirit made him angry.

"You accept it for me," I said. "You're the religious expert around here."

"You don't understand what I went through."

I said, "You never told me what you went through. All I know is what I went through."

And that comment was enough to end the fight, because in treatment they'd worked Del over good about how he had to make amends to those he'd harmed. But the only thing I needed anyone to make any amends for was something I did. *I* was the one who fucked Kevin Keel. Me. I might have gone to Kevin Keel because I was hurt and angry about Del, but it was still my choosing and my action. I had to make amends to myself for that.

"I go to church because I love you," I said. "Isn't that enough?"

Del shook his head some more at me, but he was calmed down and talked again in his Christ-voice.

"Vangie, all I remember from that day they found me was the rain pouring down in my face," he said. "I was lost."

"And now you're found?"

"I'm trying. I know you don't understand yet, but one day you will."

"Maybe," I told him, but in my heart I doubted it. The main mystery I was trying to understand was the mystery of me, Vangie, and I knew I could never learn what I needed to know in a church.

That night when we went to bed, I slept backed up against Del the way I always did, but neither of us reached for the other. All the God talk killed the desire to screw, which was a first. That more than anything convinced me of the power of religion.

I wanted nothing to do with it.

25

THE next morning I was glad to leave the house and go to the orchard to load up. Glad to leave Del. I didn't know what to do about the baby thing or the religion thing anymore, and it all made me wonder where Del and I were headed. If Del couldn't be with me when he was drinking and I couldn't be with him when he was praising God, where did that leave us?

The whole fight was still on my mind at the farmers market, and I felt unsettled and grumpy. On my way back to my stand after going to the toilet, I did something that made the day even blacker, and I did it just by stopping by the jewelry stand to look at the bits of feldspar and rose. It was my luck that a little girl was getting her ears pierced then, and even though I knew I should not stay to watch, once I saw what was happening, I couldn't leave.

The little girl hollered when her mom put her on the high stool, and she hollered as the woman who ran the booth swabbed her ears with alcohol, and she continued to holler as the woman got out her piercing gun. When the needle went into the first ear, quick like a bite, the girl squealed higher and harder, and she kept up that high, keen sound as the woman did the second ear. At the end, the little girl's eyes looked glassy because she was crying so much, and her ears were bright red from the tops down to the buds where the earrings were. That's all those lobes were, buds, because the girl was only two or so. When the lady held a mirror up so the little girl could see, the kid didn't even look. She just hid in her mother's neck.

The whole thing made me sick, because I thought the stand was probably dirty, and I didn't like the fat woman doing the piercing, with her fat arms and the rolls of her belly straining at the front of her dress. I hated the mother because I thought if you had a kid, you should wait until she asked to have her ears pierced, because then she'd know the pain was for something. At two or three, this kid couldn't know. She had to get those bits of metal in her ears because her mom wanted them.

But I was never going to have a kid, so the whole thing was beside the point. Even thinking it was beside the point. Yet there I was, thinking it, and that made me feel even blacker. I did not ever want to grow up if it meant taking the side of people like that fat woman or the little girl's mom. I had a job, I paid rent, I wanted no one to tell me what to do — but that was all I wanted of adulthood. I did not want it to be up to me to change diapers or cook meals from the four food groups or get someone's ears pierced. I did not want to take care of anyone but me.

Maybe it was the black mood I was in, and maybe it was because I didn't want to go home and get preached at, but all I could think was how much I wanted to go get stoned with June. I missed her, and I was beginning to see that even if I still felt embarrassed about telling her I wanted to be her boyfriend, feeling stupid or uncomfortable was still better than the blankness of not talking to her. That feeling just grew during the day, so after work I called her. It was the first time I'd dialed her number since the day she told me about the picture of Ray and Luke.

"Long time no see," she said when she heard me. "No hear, either. How's it hanging?"

"It's about hung," I said, and she laughed. I could hear in her voice that she was hurt because we hadn't been speaking, but she was not so hurt that she would not talk to me.

"Things are that good, huh?"

"Things are that good," I said.

"What's going on?"

"Nothing. Everything. It's a long story."

"I'll listen."

"Can I come out?" I said. "Are you busy?"

"Everyone's gone. Come on."

"Do you have any weed?"

She laughed then and said, "I always have weed."

Just hearing her say that and hearing her voice — a little husky, a little loose-sounding — made me feel better. Whatever else was going on, whatever had happened between the two of us, I knew we would be able to sit at the kitchen table, get high, and laugh. There was something easygoing in June, and that fast I knew how much and how bad I missed her.

Out at the house, it was the same scene with the dogs as the other time, with them almost knocking me down, so Lucky and Pearl got locked up again. When June and I went into the kitchen, I saw that she'd been rolling joints.

"This is for us to smoke now," she said, pointing to the water bong with her chin. "And these are for you to take with." She pushed three joints toward me then, over the tabletop.

"How much do I owe you?"

"A dollar."

"For three joints? You're crazy."

"It's for you," June said. That's when I knew it was a gift and not a transaction, and that we had forgiven each other for whatever happened.

"I see you're wearing that," I said then, because when June pushed the joints toward me, I saw she had on the ring Ray gave her.

"I wear it most of the time now."

"What's it mean?"

"It means it's easier for everyone if I wear it."

"That's all?"

"That's all," she said, holding the smoke in. "What about you? Does Del ever talk about putting a ring on your finger?"

The question seemed strange to me. Even if I had a ring from Del, it would be nothing like her taking a ring from Ray at the same time she was screwing Luke. We couldn't just be two girls sitting around talking about when we might get married.

"Mostly Del talks about knocking me up."

"Are you going to do it?"

"Get pregnant? Jesus Christ, no." And that seemed strange to me, too, that I'd even have to say that to June. I said, "A baby doesn't interest me at all."

"It might interest me if I was with the right person. I might want a baby then."

That surprised me. It didn't seem at all like her. But I didn't say, *Well, who's the right person,* or *How are you going to be able to tell whose baby it is?* I wasn't there to fight or preach. So instead I went, "Well, I wish you luck with all of that. With choosing, I mean."

"The choice is made," she said. "You know that, don't you, Vangie?"

I didn't know how the choice could be made when she was still in the house with the two of them, but I nodded. I knew she wanted me to. She waited a few seconds before she said the next thing.

"It felt good when it started. Now it just seems complicated. The lies are getting more complicated. But I don't lie to you, Vangie, and I never did. At least not for long."

I said, "No, you didn't lie for long."

"The next time you see me, things aren't going to be like this."

She looked around the room when she said that, and I thought that's what she meant: that the three of them weren't going to be living in that house much longer, that she was going to make a move. She didn't say that, but I was sure she meant that.

She passed the bong back to me then, and that's when I looked past the ring and saw her fingers. Each one was bitten down to the quick of the nail. They looked like baby fingers, all pink and without even the thinnest thread of white nail showing. When I saw that, I knew I had no idea, really, of how things were with her.

"You know more about me than anyone, Vangie," she said then.

"More than Luke?"

"Probably. You know different things about me, Vangie. You know me longer, too."

I could tell by the way she kept saying my name that she was high, high, high.

"You know me pretty well, too," I said.

We stopped talking then, and June filled the bong a second time. The ticking of the clock and the whirring of the refrigerator seemed loud, the way they always did when I was stoned. To keep from staring at June's fingers as she packed in the pot, I studied the kitchen table. Along with salt and pepper shakers and a napkin holder that I remembered us making in seventh grade shop class, two bottles of

Jim Beam were out on the table. There were a few glasses with the whiskey, and it looked like it was just where the three of them kept it. Handy-like.

"Do you know what's funny?" June said then.

"What?" I said. "What's funny?"

"It's funny you and I never kissed. I thought so many times when we were talking, Vangie, that we'd kiss. But we never did."

I looked at her after she said that, and she looked like herself, but she also looked like a stranger. She was someone I loved and did not know at all. It was the way my mother looked to me right before she left, and the way Del looked when he came home from treatment. Strangers all the more strange because I loved them.

"I didn't know you thought about that," I said.

"Didn't you ever think about it?"

It was the first time in a long time that I wanted to tell the truth, or what I knew of the truth.

"No," I said. "Or if I did think of it, I didn't know it."

"It's all right," she said. "It doesn't hurt my feelings if you didn't think about it."

We sat there, not talking, and I felt the same way I felt the night I told her I wanted to be her boyfriend — even though she was the one who spoke, who said words that couldn't be taken back. I thought we would go on sitting there, not talking, but June said the next thing. Took the next chance.

"Do you want to kiss now?" she said.

I didn't answer, but I didn't move when she got up from

the chair or when she smoothed a piece of my hair back from my face.

"Hey friend," she said. Then we were kissing.

It was not like any kiss I ever had. There was no insistence in it, no next step. Her mouth tasted cloudy. When June made a small noise into the kiss, I did, too.

"It's hard," she said when she pulled away. "Both of us wanting to be the girl."

I didn't say anything. I didn't know what to say. If there had been a time to kiss, it was the night I told her I wanted to be her boyfriend. But I had backed up a million miles from that place. I could not keep letting her touch me.

"Do you ever think about leaving, Vangie? Going some-place else and starting over?"

"All the time."

She told me again that the next time I saw her, things would be different, even though she really did love Ray. Then she told me about the kind thing Ray had done for her. I was hardly there and could hardly hear the things she was saying, but I made myself listen.

When her allergies were bad at the end of the summer and her eyes burned and itched, Ray would make her lie down on the bed, and he'd put his mouth over each of her eyes. He'd lick gently at each lid, at the little bit of red rim, and at the eyeball itself.

"He said that his mom used to do it for him when he was little, whenever he got something in his eye. He said it always made him feel better."

"And that's why you love him."

"That's not the only reason," she said. "But what you said before? About how it can't go on? I know it. I keep meaning to leave. And I don't."

And even though I was hardly there in the room with her anymore, I made myself say, "You can leave anytime you want to."

I said it, but I didn't believe it. I believed things were the way they were with Ray and Luke because June wanted them to be that way. She was right in the middle, at the center, and she didn't want to swim to shore. Just as I was thinking that, Luke walked in.

"What's this?" he said when he came into the room. From the way he looked at me, I knew he was trying to read my face, but I pulled that door closed. He stood watching us awhile, then he walked toward the table and reached for one of the bottles of Jim Beam.

"Guess I'll join the party," he said, but I was already pushing back from the table.

"Stay," June said to me. "My two favorite people. I want you two to be friends."

I said, "Luke already is my friend."

"I always tell him you're like a sister to me, Vangie. No, I tell him we're closer than sisters. I told him you know everything."

"I don't know everything."

"You know everything about us," June said, and even though she was talking to me, she was looking at Luke when she said it. I could tell from the way her arm shifted that she was touching him under the table. Rubbing his thigh and cock.

"I bet you hear more than you ever wanted to," I said to Luke.

"No. But I hear a lot. See a lot, too."

When he said that, his face went cold, and I knew I wasn't the only one in the room who could shut the door tight on what was inside.

"You've been a stranger out here," he said then. "Have a drink?"

He was reaching for another glass, but he wasn't asking me to stay. It was all a sign that I should keep on moving and become the stranger he just called me. I wondered when he'd come home and how long he'd been standing outside the kitchen, looking in at June and me. Long enough to see our kiss and all that sisterly affection was my guess. I stood up.

"It's good night for me," I said.

"All right, if we can't persuade you," June said, and downed the shot Luke had poured for her. Then she pushed the three joints toward me.

I said, "I'll have to hide them."

"Del doesn't party at all anymore?"

"Not at all."

"What does he do with himself?"

"He found religion."

"Oh, Jesus." June laughed. "Well, don't worry. That will never rub off on you, Vangie. You're as fucked up as I am."

"I guess."

"Well, say 'hey' to him for me."

"I will," I told her, though I had no intention of saying

her name. Luke was into his second shot of Jim Beam when I nodded to him. Then I was out the door.

On the way home, I did not let myself think about anything except the road. It had been a long time since I drove high. After a couple miles I rolled the window down all the way, took the three joints from the car seat, and held them up over the car so the wind would take them. I guess I could have saved them for a rainy day, but I wanted nothing to do with the kind of comfort or stupidity they brought. I didn't want anything she gave me.

I knew I was angry with June, but it was hard to think through all the reasons. I didn't like what she'd said to me, and I didn't like what she was doing out at that house. It all seemed so easy for her. The two of them in love with her, and her just taking it all in, like it was her due. And to top it all off, bringing me into it, too. Fuck her, I thought.

I didn't know if Kevin fucked her when she was a kid or if she was still trying to live out that story, but I was done trying to analyze and understand. I didn't care why she was with Ray and Luke, I didn't care that she used to think about kissing me. I didn't want to be part of it anymore. That was clear in my mind as I drove the black roads home.

THAT NIGHT when Del came home from the three-to-eleven shift, I was already in bed. I was still high, but I'd washed the marijuana smoke out of my hair. I was such an old hand at pretending to be straight, I knew I could blame any oddness on being tired.

When Del slid into bed behind me, his skin felt warm and

damp from his shower, and I knew if the light was on, I'd see where the shower had turned his skin red. He didn't say anything and neither did I, but as he settled in behind me and draped one arm over me, I reached back for his cock, which was smooth and warm from the shower. I could feel him go alert, but he still didn't say anything, and I kept grasping and holding until he was hard in my hand and I could run my palm over him and play with the hard-soft ridge of his head. I did that for a while, and then I let go so I could turn in the bed.

"I thought you were sleeping."

"I'm awake now," I said.

I kept pulling and tugging, and soon there was a little bit of wetness at the end of him.

I said, "Can you tell I want something from you?"

"Can you tell I want to give you something?"

I moved my legs apart then so he could get his fingers up into me, and we lay like that, each of us working the other.

"I want to open you up, Vangie," he said then, and I knew what he meant. It always hurt a little when he did it, but I liked it, too.

"Can I open up your pussy?"

"Go ahead, honey," I said, and I stopped touching his cock and lay facedown on the bed and let him pull a pillow under my hips.

That night, just like the other times he tried, he could only get his hand inside me up to his knuckles. His bones wouldn't give and neither would mine, no matter how much jelly we used. But he'd get in far enough that he could rub the muscles deep inside me, by my cervix, and the whole thing would hurt and feel good at the same time. It hurt to have the bones of his hand pushing into me, and it felt like my skin was raw from the rubbing, but I loved being touched so deep inside.

"There's the nose," he said, because that's what my cervix felt like to him, and he kept touching it with the tip of his finger.

"Make yourself come, Vangie. Open up for me."

I had to push up against my own weight to even get my hand between my legs, and then I had to hold myself up a little on one shoulder so I could rub. It made the blood pound in my head, but I knew it wouldn't take me long to come, so I did it.

When I was close, I said, "I'll come on your hand."

"Do it. I want to feel it."

I came hard. Del kept his hand deep in me for some of it, then he got inside me as fast as he could so he could feel the last bit on his cock.

"I want to put some come right up there," he said. "Right up there."

It felt like the inside of me was on fire, and when Del started to come, I felt it before I heard him. I could tell by the way he grunted and shook that he came hard, too.

"Those are some strong muscles," he said when he was done, when we were just lying there. "You made my hand ache."

"You made the inside of me ache," I said.

"Was it too much?"

"Almost," I said. "Just almost."

He didn't say anything about a baby or me going off the pill, and I didn't say anything about his God talk. That night I needed a fuck hard enough to make me ache, and Del gave it to me. What he got from me I couldn't say, but for the moment it seemed that my body and heart were enough.

26

THE next morning was Wednesday, so I did not have to work at all and Del did not have to work until three. We were asleep when the knocking started, and it took me a while to even hear it, because I blended it into my dream. Sometimes my dad came by for a cup of coffee on the mornings he knew I was going out to the market, so I figured it was him and that he'd forgotten my days off.

"Who the fuck is it?" Del said when he saw me pull the bedroom curtain aside and look outside.

"My dad. Go back to sleep."

I pulled on my red kimono, and that's when I looked at the clock. Five a.m. Early even for my dad. And then I figured something was wrong, and I got wide awake, just like that.

"I woke you, didn't I," my dad said when I opened the back door.

"It's all right," I said. "Is everything okay with mom?"

"I assume so. I haven't heard from her."

So my heart stopped pounding quite so hard. I stepped into the kitchen so my dad could come in and close the door. The morning air was cold on my ankles. I had no idea why he was there at five in the morning, but for all I knew he'd been up all night drinking. You never knew with my dad.

"Coffee?" I said.

"If you're making it."

"Now I am."

"That kimono reminds me of the one I brought your mother from Korea," he said. "Pure silk."

He pronounced the word as if it were spelled k-i-m-o-n-a.

"This is satin," I said.

"Same difference." Then my dad said, "That's your friend living out there with those Sparrow boys, isn't it? That Keel girl."

"June?"

"That's her name. I couldn't remember. Well, she was on — they all were on — the police scanner last night."

He told me what he knew. As soon as he said the words, I could see it happening. I'd been out to the house. I knew where the bedrooms were, and I knew where the gun was.

I guess something showed on my face, because my dad said, "Did you know something about it?"

I shook my head. "Some of it," I said.

"The younger boy was the one they flew out of there. He was pretty bad off," my dad said. "Do you want to drive out?"

"Just let me put real clothes on," I said.

Upstairs I pulled on jeans and a shirt, boots but no socks. I could feel ridges of leather under my toes. My mouth was dry. I left Del sleeping in the bed.

My dad and I drove all the hilly roads of Mennonite Town without seeing one car, but when we got close to the house, there were other people on the road. No one could see anything, though: two cruisers were there, and they had the place blocked off. All we could do was drive on by.

"She's over to the hospital, I'm sure," my dad said. "She's all right, Vangie."

When I still didn't say anything, he went, "Come out to the house and give a listen on the scanner. I'm sure someone will be talking."

On the way to my dad's house my mind was working a hundred details and I had a sick feeling in my stomach. I kept thinking about the .38 Special and the night I didn't want to sleep beside it. I wanted to tell my dad something about the gun, but I didn't know what to say. I was worried that once I told one story, I'd have to tell another. Some I could tell and it would be all right, and others I could never tell. All the stories bled together in my mind.

My dad seemed to understand what I was going through, because he didn't make me talk. We watched the road and the houses beside it, and the truck itself was like a moving room, filled with my dad's thoughts and my own. The whole way to his place, neither of us said a thing. Or if we did, I don't remember.

2 7

My dad was right when he told me Ray was the one airlifted out. It didn't make any difference — he died on the way to Deer Run. His problems started before he ever got in the air, though, before he was ever put on that helicopter. People said he pretty much bled to death at the house. Gunshot wound to the stomach. I learned that a few hours after it happened. It took a couple of days to hear the rest.

Ray must have known what he was looking for that night, because he parked his car up on the road and walked down to the house. He was already carrying the shotgun when he walked down — he left the open box of shells on his car seat. He walked down to the house carrying the loaded shotgun, and the dogs didn't bark because they knew him. He walked in on June and Luke. Saw them. That was the moment I kept imagining. June's stomach must have caught fire when the door opened and light from the hall-way poured into the room. Or maybe June and Luke made love with the lights on, and Ray stood watching for a while.

Ray shot Luke in the chest, and then he went after June. He dragged her into the hall, kicked her until her arm and cheekbone broke. She must have had her arm up in front of her face. He almost took her eye out, and then I guess he had enough, because he kicked her down the stairs. She had to lie there at the bottom of the stairwell and listen while he went after Luke a second time. By then, though, Luke had gotten to the pistol.

The whole thing probably lasted three or four minutes. It probably seemed like a long time to the three of them.

It took sixty-two stitches to close June's eye and cheek and scalp. They had to wire her cheekbone together. No one blamed Ray — he was dead, and he was the wronged one anyway. Luke took the brunt of the gossip. I heard it. He was the blood relative, and no one could forgive him for that.

I heard that when the ambulance came, Luke and June were lying at the bottom of the stairs, just a blanket over them. I could believe that. But then someone tried to tell me that when the paramedics went to lift June onto the gur-ney, they saw come running down her leg, and I stopped listening.

Neither June nor Luke mentioned me at the grand jury. Neither of them placed me at the house that night. I don't know why. Maybe they didn't want to mention the weed. Maybe June wanted to protect me. Maybe it just didn't make any difference that I was there.

At the hearing the attorney made a fuss about the Jim Beam and how all three had been drinking that night — June and Luke at home, and Ray out at the Ruby. I could have told them that whatever happened that night didn't happen because of whiskey. It might have been helped along by whiskey, but it was something that started a long time ago — when Luke and Ray were kids, or when June was still at home with her brothers. Who knew. But even if someone had asked me, I guess I wouldn't have told them what I thought anyway. It wasn't mine to tell.

The grand jury determined that Luke fired only after being fired upon, and only in self-defense. There was no premeditation. Some people thought it was a fair ruling because of all the loss already involved for the family, and others, like Del, thought it was no ruling at all. I thought it was as fair as anything that wasn't going to bring Ray back.

I didn't tell Del anything about the night Ray was killed. I didn't tell him that I'd been out to the house, or that I'd smoked with June. None of it. All I told him was that I knew June loved Ray. I told him the story she told me that last night. I didn't say when I heard it, just that I had.

"And that's why she loved him, because he put his tongue on her eye?" Del said when I was done talking. "That's the only reason why?"

"I don't think it's the only reason. It's just what she picked to tell me."

"Fucking-A, Vangie, that's the fucking stupidest thing I ever heard. He cared for her. He wanted to marry her."

"I know he did."

"How could you be friends with her? Couldn't you see what a piece of shit she was?"

"She wasn't that," I said. "You didn't know her."

"I don't have to know her to see what she is. A worthless piece of shit."

I didn't blame him. It was his friend who bled to death in that upstairs room.

I believed June when she told me she loved Ray. It was a mistaken love, and a selfish one, but I believed her. I understood it the way I understood what June told me about the photograph of Luke and Ray: it took me a while to see the pattern and drift of June's thoughts, but in the end I understood her flawed actions as much as I understood my own.

Even though I wasn't the one who pulled a trigger, I felt I had a certain role in Ray's death. My lie — or my unwillingness to give up June's lie — had contributed to Ray's death. It was an awful thing, thinking that. Sometimes I let myself think it and sometimes I pushed it away. I'd seen June's way of looking at things and I saw Del's way. I had to live someplace in between.

FOR ALL their gossiping and supposing, no one in all of Mahanaqua saw the next piece coming. Maybe they thought ugliness and shame would end the affair, and maybe they thought that guilt — guilt and her own scarred and pinned face — would cripple June. But none of that happened. June stayed with Luke. She stayed with him, and they moved into a house, an old abandoned cabin out on the lake road. After a couple weeks of broken windows and paint being thrown on the house, people left the two of them alone. They were pariahs. They got their privacy.

It made sense to me. Why wouldn't she turn to the person who knew her worst failings? She had to go somewhere for her love.

Once when I drove by the house, she was out on the front stoop. I blew the horn and waved. She looked up and, when she saw it was me, waved back. Her face was not bad. Swollen, the one eye a little off. Hair still short, no doubt from the stitches she had. That's all I could see as I drove by.

I should have pulled over and gotten out, but I didn't. Didn't call later. The number wasn't in the book. But the phone never rang at my place, either.

I think he is the only one who really sees her now.

2 8

I came home from work one
day all excited about this dog that had shown up at the farmers market. I didn't know what kind of dog he was and I
didn't care. He had fur the color of vanilla cake batter and
eyes like raisins. I fell in love with him from the moment I
saw him. I got the guys at the butcher counter to give him a
bone so he'd stick around. I wanted him, and I figured Del
would be excited, too, since he'd been talking about getting
a dog for some time. I did not want a baby, but I thought I
could handle a dog.

"Guess what?" I said to Del when I came in the door. It

took me only a second to see what was going on, though, and I didn't say anything about the dog after that.

Del was well into a case of Yuengling, and he had a full bottle of vodka on the coffee table as well.

"What?" he said. "What's the news?"

"Nothing, really. What's going on with you?"

"I'm having a couple drinks."

"I see. How come?"

"Should I open one for you?" he said, taking up one of the beers. It was his way of being polite: opening a bottle or can and then passing it to me.

"Sure," I said. "How come you're drinking, though?" I asked the question in my careful, cheerful voice, the one I used when Del was drinking, so it would sound like I wasn't accusing but was just being his honest-to-God, why-don't-you-tell-me-the-truth friend.

"I needed a break."

"Did you go to work?"

"Called in. Told them I was sick."

"Well, that happens," I said. "What did you need a break from?"

He kind of rolled his head off to one side and said, "All this goddamn treatment shit. I'm sick of it. And I'm sick of that goddamn church shit. Hell, you might as well be in hell, the way they want you to live."

He sat quiet after that, staring off into space, and I didn't say anything. I also didn't say anything when he went for the vodka and cracked the seal on it. I didn't know what to say anyway. What was going to happen was going to happen.

After he pulled down three or four mouthfuls straight from the bottle, I said, "Hey, why don't you save some of that for me."

He stopped slugging and passed the bottle over to me.

And I did take a swallow. Then I stood up and picked up the bottle to take into the kitchen with me. I said, "Want some dinner?"

"I want some pussy."

"Did you eat all day?"

"I'll eat you."

I put the vodka in the broom closet where he would not think to look for it. When I went back into the living room I sat beside Del and kissed him because it was easier than talking. I knew the routine.

"Take off your clothes," he said. "Get out those tits."

"Do you want to go upstairs and lie down?"

"I want to fuck your cunt right here."

While I was standing beside the sofa getting undressed, and while he was sitting on the sofa with his cock in his hand, waiting for me, I kept thinking something would happen that would change everything. But nothing happened. I went on taking off my clothes, and he went on holding his erection.

"I stink," I said.

"I want to fuck you, not smell you."

"Okay," I said. "If you don't want to wait for me to shower."

"I don't want to wait."

I was just climbing onto him on the sofa when he said, "And I threw out your fucking pills."

I stopped for one second, then I just went on lowering myself onto him.

"So I guess you think you're going to knock me up," I said.

"I'm going to fuck you up right now."

I didn't bother to tell him that it would take a while before the pill got out of my system, that some women had to wait a couple months before their bodies got back to normal. If he didn't know that, it was his problem.

"If I waited for you to get rid of them, I'd be waiting forever."

He told me then that I wouldn't find them in the trash either, so there was no point in looking.

After we fucked for a while, Del pulled out of me so he could put some spit on his cock. I guess I was dry. Before he got back inside, he grabbed me between my legs and squeezed.

"I want you to shave your pussy, too," he said.

When I didn't say anything, he said, "I want you to shave your pussy bald for me."

I thought of saying no or getting up from the sofa or pushing him away, but it was easier to stay there.

"Sure," I said. "Tomorrow."

"I been wanting that awhile," he said. "I want to fuck a bald pussy."

"Are you going to fuck me now?" I asked.

"Do you want to get your pussy fucked?"

"Sure," I said. "Go ahead."

So he got back up inside me and he screwed me, and I almost didn't feel a thing.

THE NEXT morning, I lay in bed when Del got up and got himself ready for work. Before he went downstairs, he came and stood beside the bed.

"You all right, Vangie?"

He waited there in the half-light for me to answer, but I didn't say anything. When he leaned down to kiss me, I didn't move.

"I gotta go," he said.

After I heard his car pull away, I still stayed in bed. I heard the cardinal call, and I lay listening to that. My vagina felt swollen from all the fucking, and there was a little raw place just inside my lips, right by the opening. After we made it upstairs to the bedroom, Del shoved the dildo and his cock into my vagina at the same time, and I figured that's what made the raw place. He'd fucked me in the cunt and ass and mouth and back again, and I had the smell of everything on me and in me. I brushed my teeth in the middle of the night, but I let everything else sit until morning.

So I made myself get up, and I made myself take a bath. I washed inside myself with watery fingers. After I got out of the tub, I put hydrogen peroxide on my breasts. Pieces of me burned, but that was better. At least I felt clean.

BY THE time Del came home from work, I had myself packed and my bags loaded in the truck. I didn't leave when he was working. I wasn't a coward.

When he saw me standing beside my truck with all my shit piled in it, he looked as surprised as anyone who didn't know a thing was wrong. He said, "What the hell, Vangie, what the hell?"

"I can't do it anymore."

"What are you talking about? What can't you do?"

"This," I said, and motioned to the house. "Us."

"You can pour the vodka down the drain. I'll get back on track."

"That's not it."

"What is it? Is it the pills?"

"It's not just the pills."

"Then what the hell?"

I didn't feel like saying the word *dildo* in the daylight, and I didn't feel like saying, *I don't like the taste of my own shit.* He'd put his cock in my mouth after fucking me in the ass last night, but he probably didn't even remember doing it. So I told Del the one thing I knew to say, that I remembered from the day my mom left my dad.

I said, "It is never just one thing."

I unbuttoned my shirt and pulled my bra over to show him the new black places on my breasts, the ones he bit into me when we were on the sofa. He'd broken the skin twice, and those places were the sorest. I had little bandages on them over the breaks in the skin, but there was still plenty of black blood showing through my skin.

"I don't need such beautiful bruises," I said.

"It wasn't my intention to hurt you."

"I know," I said. "Intentionally you love me."

It went on a while longer, but there's no point in repeating the words. Just as I was getting into the truck, though, Del said one thing that, while it did not change what was happening at that moment, changed everything that had happened before — all of our time together.

"I knew you fucked him, Vangie," he said. "But it doesn't matter. It never did."

For a second I thought he was talking about Kevin Keel, and then I realized it was not the latest lie he was talking about but the old one.

"Frank told me that night," Del said. "He couldn't wait to tell me."

I let his words sink in. They wrapped themselves in my hair and fell tingling and burning on my skin.

"Why didn't you ever say anything to me?"

"What was there to say? It was done."

"Didn't it bother you?"

"Sure it bothered me. Then I didn't care."

"You didn't care at all?"

"I didn't know why you did it," Del said. "But I knew I didn't want it to matter. It didn't change anything between you and me."

By the way he said it, I could tell he believed it. And maybe it hadn't mattered. Maybe he loved me exactly the way he would have loved me even if I hadn't fucked Frank. Maybe Frank wasn't the reason Del bit black bruises into my skin. Maybe Del really didn't care that I was the biggest liar that walked the earth. And maybe Del was just trying to give me what he thought I wanted when he shoved his cock and dildo up inside me at the same time: two cocks. I didn't know.

"It happened one time, Vangie. It wasn't like June and Ray."

"No, it wasn't like June and Ray," I said, but all I had to do was look at Del's face to see the truth. That was my piece of the devastation.

"If I could, I would take it all back, Del. I would never hurt you like that."

"Right," he said, and looked away. Then he shook his head and looked back at me.

"I thought," he said, "that we were really working on something here."

"I thought, too. I just don't know what."

I was crying by then, and so was he.

"And you don't think a kid would change that," he said.

"I don't think a baby would change that."

I didn't know anymore why I was leaving, but I couldn't make myself want to stay. There was a huge difference between those two things, though, and I knew it. I had to know. My life depended on it.

29

O<small>F</small> course there was no phone hooked up in the kitchenette anymore, so I drove into town to use the pay phone at the gas station. I could have gone to my dad's to make a call, but this was one I had to make from the privacy of the street. I had a fistful of change, and my hand was shaking as I dumped in the coins. I didn't call collect.

"It's me, Vangie," I said when my mom picked up. Besides my dad, she was the one other person I was bound to. No one else was left.

"It's your long-lost daughter," I said.

"Your long-lost mother is more like it. I haven't been very good about keeping in touch. How are you, honey?"

"I'm doing all right," I said. "I can't talk long. I just wanted to call and say I'm single again. Del and I broke up."

"Oh Evangeline," my mom said then. But I give her credit. She didn't try to sound wise or make me feel better.

"I'm sorry, honey. Do you want to talk about it?"

"Not particularly. I just wanted to let you know where I was. I'll be at the apartment for a while."

"Well, I appreciate the phone call. I like to hear from you."

"It goes both ways," I said. "How are you?"

"I'm fine. I'm always fine," my mom said. Then she went, "Be careful, Vangie. You don't want to have a life like mine."

I said, "I don't know whose life I want to have."

"Are you sure you don't want to tell me more about what happened, honey?"

"It wasn't just one thing, Ma. I can't talk about it."

"I understand."

That was all. There were other things I could have told her — about Del, about Kevin Keel. Even some things about June. But it wasn't really my mom I wanted to tell those things to.

It took three weeks for that set of bruises to disappear. Like any scar, they told a story. They embarrassed me, but I was sorry to see them fade.

ACKNOWLEDGMENTS

Thank you to:

Nicole and Sarah, for taking a chance; David, for the photograph; Mary, for always picking up; Loyda, for the cabin; Jim, for taking time at Iowa and years after; Tom, for all the sword-fish dinners on the terrace; Lynn, for chai and proofing; Richard, for being an early, enthusiastic reader; Melodee, for introducing me to Blue (and the dump); Jeff, for enduring.

Swimming Sweet Arrow
by Maureen Gibbon

A READING GROUP GUIDE

"Here is what they never tell you about being a girl."

A Conversation with Maureen Gibbon

An obvious component of Swimming Sweet Arrow *is the explicit sexuality. What did you hope to achieve through this explicitness?*

I think many women have the sexual feelings and experiences that my protagonist Vangie has, but those things aren't always discussed openly. That's part of what the sentence "Here is what they never tell you about being a girl" is about. I didn't want things to stay polite in this story, so I pushed myself to let Vangie say things that were hard to say. I wanted her to be able to speak bluntly and specifically about the things that compel her. The result is sometimes raw. Sex isn't the only thing Vangie is explicit about, though. She's also explicit in the ways she describes her jobs — carrying chickens, waiting tables, and picking pears. All of her jobs are very physical, and I hope those descriptions are no less vivid or detailed.

Your book invites the reader into the bedroom (or backseat) of the main character, and it almost demands a kind of intimacy on the part of the reader. What kinds of reactions have you gotten?

That the book is daring. That the sex is enthusiastic, and that there is a joyousness in the frankness of it all. A couple people have read it all at one sitting. All kinds of things.

Did you feel that you had crossed over some kind of line in writing so explicitly?

Sure, I often felt I crossed the line. A few places in the book are still hard for me to look at. But once I started being that direct and specific, it was hard to be anything but that. Vangie's voice became the standard.

You commented earlier on Vangie's jobs, all of which you write about very knowledgeably. Have you worked as a waitress, pear picker, or chicken carrier?

I did all those jobs as I was growing up. They all made a very strong impression on me, and I've never been able to forget them. It makes sense to me, because when you learn a job, you take in a lot of information that you need to know, and if the job involves any manual work, you take in information with your body, too. My body remembers picking pears, carrying chickens, waitressing. It also remembers the very visceral details of those workplaces. I like to write about work because I like to describe the actions and processes of it, and how the person moves through the work. There's a lot of beauty in it to me, even if it's a bad or taxing job. I've also worked as a church secretary and as a change girl in a casino, but I haven't written about those jobs yet.

Of Vangie's jobs, which was your personal favorite?

Picking pears was the hardest but the most beautiful because of the green fruit and trees. Carrying chickens was not as bad as you'd assume it to be, in spite of the chicken shit. Waitressing produced the greatest number of nightmares and feelings of dread, but I remember that job best of all and feel some strange sort of love for its details. I still have one of my old green "Guest Check" pads.

Do you believe it enriches a writer's work to have those kinds of jobs?

Many American writers have thought that for a long time, and I respect and embrace the tradition. Yet I say that from a position of luxury, because I don't have to do those jobs now to earn a living. I don't know what would have happened to me if I hadn't gone on to college and moved into the wider world. I don't know if I would be calling those jobs enriching then.

There are tremendously deep friendships in Swimming Sweet Arrow — *and tremendous betrayals. Can you talk about those themes of friendship and fidelity?*

I didn't think about themes as I was writing, but you're right, there are certainly deep betrayals between different characters. The question makes me think of a poem by Marina Tsvetaeva where she writes about how sometimes, when we are being utterly faithless to others, we are being true to ourselves. I believe that. At the same time, you don't want just to go around damaging people, or acting wholly out of self-interest. That's no life either. I'd say that Vangie has awareness of that distinction. And she knows herself, or is trying to know herself and the behavior of which she's capable.

Any plans for a second book?

Absolutely. I'm in the gathering stage right now, letting voices and images come and go. I can't say more than that. It's good to be at this place. I don't want to jinx it.

———————

Reading Group Questions
and Topics for Discussion

1. What are the forces that, in the absence of parental or other adult guidance, help Vangie determine the kind of person she wants to be? What fuels her frustration when, at the end of the novel, she tells her mother, "I don't know whose life I want to have"?

2. None of Vangie's jobs is very enviable, but she derives a strong sense of self and purpose from them. Why? What do Vangie's jobs teach her about the world? About herself? Why is the most physically demanding job — picking pears — described in almost poetic terms?

3. Maureen Gibbon's writing has been likened to that of Kate Chopin, Anaïs Nin, and Colette because of its frank exploration of female sexuality. What do Vangie and June have in common with the characters created by Chopin, Colette, and Nin? Why do you think sexually forthright women characters in fiction continue to cause such a stir?

4. At the beginning of Chapter 2, Vangie states that there is a great deal "they never tell you about being a girl." How does this lack of information affect Vangie? Can Vangie gain the knowledge she seeks through means

other than hard experience? Do girls today confront a comparable lack of access to information?

5. When Vangie reflects on June's involvement with two brothers, she states that "none of us did anything for long unless we wanted to." What is Vangie saying here about choice? About self-knowledge? Are there other instances in the novel where Vangie seems to struggle to understand herself or her own role in an event?

6. What is the significance of Vangie's dream of the owl at the end of chapter 17? How does her experience of this dream contrast with Del's interpretation of the dream in chapter 24? Why does Vangie reject the religious devotion that seems to bring Del such comfort?

7. Del makes a valiant effort to rehabilitate himself after his overdose and seems to cleave to the principles of a twelve-step program. What undermines his efforts to change?

8. How would you characterize the relationship between Vangie and June? Why does Vangie turn away from June at the end of the book, at a moment when her friendship would have probably been particularly important to June? What does Vangie mean in chapter 25 when she says, "I could not keep letting [June] touch me"?

9. After tremendous intimacy and friendship, Del and June are still "strangers" to Vangie, "all the more strange because I loved them," she says. What is Vangie saying here about the nature of love?

10. Although Vangie makes numerous missteps over the course of the novel, she also takes certain steps to expand her world and to increase the number of choices she has. Identify some of those steps. Is Vangie a character who is bound to be determined by her environment, or are there hints that she will go beyond the limited world of Mahanaqua?

11. The characters in *Swimming Sweet Arrow* seem to talk more easily about explicit sexual acts than about virtually anything else. While the physicality of the sex in the novel cannot be denied, how does sex also serve as a metaphor in *Swimming Sweet Arrow*?

12. What is the role of the water imagery in the novel? Besides the title, where else does it occur?

13. Why is it important to Vangie to tell this story? Why does she struggle until she can say, "There. Now it is all written down"?

Maureen Gibbon's suggestions for further reading

The Professor's House
by Willa Cather

The Awakening
by Kate Chopin

The Lover
by Marguerite Duras

The Nick Adams Stories
by Ernest Hemingway

The Diviners
by Margaret Laurence

So Long, See You Tomorrow
by William Maxwell

Lives of Girls and Women

by Alice Munro

Train Whistle Guitar

by Albert Murray

The Atlas

by William T. Vollman

Winter Wheat

by Margaret Walker

Maureen Gibbon's suggestions for viewing

Each of these films is currently available on video.

Desert Bloom

Gas, Food, Lodging

Ruby in Paradise

The Boys of My Youth
by Jo Ann Beard

"Utterly compelling . . . uncommonly beautiful. . . . Life in these pages is an astonishment. . . . *The Boys of My Youth* speaks volumes about growing up female and struggling to remain true to yourself."
— Dan Cryer, *Newsday*

"Reading Jo Ann Beard's prose feels as comfortable as falling into step beside an old, intimate friend. . . . She remembers (or imagines) her childhood self with an uncanny lucidity that startles."
— Laura Miller, *New York Times Book Review*

Dale Loves Sophie to Death
by Robb Forman Dew

Winner of the National Book Award

"A novel that profoundly satisfies both the mind and the heart."
— Robert Wilson, *Washington Post Book World*

"Like Virginia Woolf, Robb Forman Dew reaches into the flow of daily life to break open a single moment. She captures beautifully the shift and flux of feelings, friendships, perspectives, the child in the adult and adult in the child."
— Jean Strouse, *Newsweek*

BACK BAY BOOKS

Available wherever books are sold

Sonny Liston Was a Friend of Mine
by Thom Jones

"True to form as one of literature's practicing wild men of prose, Thom Jones delivers a collection that is a nutty perfection of the weird and the wasted, done to wondrous effect.... Jones is a brilliant risk taker whose stories reward you with their ornery, out-there energy." — *Elle*

"This might be Jones's best work yet, which is saying something, since *The Pugilist at Rest* was a National Book Award finalist.... The stories in *Sonny Liston Was a Friend of Mine* snap and crackle like high-tension wires." — William Porter, *Denver Post*

The Power of the Dog
by Thomas Savage
with an afterword by Annie Proulx

"Thomas Savage is a writer of the first order, and he possesses in abundance the novelist's highest art — the ability to illuminate and move." — *The New Yorker*

"*The Power of the Dog* offers so many pleasures readers will be forgiven if they do not immediately notice that it also engages the grandest themes — among them, the dynamics of family, the varieties of love, and the ethos of the American West. Put simply, *The Power of the Dog* is a masterpiece." — Larry Watson, author of *Montana 1948* and *Justice*

Available wherever books are sold

Make Believe
by Joanna Scott

"Wonderful. . . . There are things in *Make Believe* that take the breath away. . . . One cannot help urging anyone who loves writing to read this book."
— Nick Hornby, *New York Times Book Review*

"There's something particularly magical when a full-fledged grown-up author is able to tell a story as if the words were coming directly, innocently, from the mouth or mind of a child."
— Patrick T. Reardon, *Chicago Tribune*

Evening News
by Marly Swick

"An affecting novel . . . utterly palpable and real. . . . It possesses both the psychological suspense of Sue Miller's bestselling *The Good Mother* and the emotional acuity of Alice Munro's short stories."
— Michiko Kakutani, *New York Times*

"A novel that might be lifted right out of the headlines — a story of a family shattered by loss when a nine-year-old accidentally shoots his half sister. . . . A book that lingers in the mind and heart."
— Colleen Kelly Warren, *St. Louis Post-Dispatch*

Available wherever books are sold